SPECTRE 2:

a collection of ghost stories
chosen by RICHARD DAVIS

Abelard
London

And this one is for
Mark Jacobs

ISBN 0 200 72389 8

Abelard-Schuman Limited
450 Edgware Road
London W2
and
Kingswood House
Heath and Reach
Leighton Buzzard
Bedfordshire

Reproduced, printed and bound in Great Britain by
Morrison & Gibb Ltd., London and Edinburgh

SPECTRE 2:

a collection of ghost stories

Contents

Acknowledgment

Grateful thanks to Harvey Unna Ltd for permission to include "The Tall Woman" by Rosemary Timperley.

Introduction

Here is the second in a series of collections of supernatural tales. There is a slight difference between this one and the first *Spectre*, in that while the previous collection included several stories which had been published before, all the material in the following pages except "The Judge's House" appears definitely for the first time ever.

Another slight difference between *Spectre 2* and its predecessor is that, while *Spectre 1* included tales that were designed to lighten the tension, and in some cases even to make you laugh, the accent here is firmly on the more spine-chilling aspects of the ghost story. We would be very interested to know whether you prefer your ghosts to be really terrifying, or in the lighter, more comic vein. Or both.

We start off this little brew with a story which is well in the traditional rattle-of-chains mould. Descended from the type of tale which our grandparents were believed to have told round the crackling log fire at Christmas (I wonder if they *really* did?), its deliberately tongue-in-cheek title sets the mood. It might make you think twice before sitting down to do a jigsaw puzzle: you too might be putting together slightly more than you bargained for . . .

The same applies to the leading character in our second piece, the more enigmatically titled "TA/9/73" — though he thoroughly deserves all he gets. His joke shop stocks more than just harmless, if rather cruel, practical jokes. Conjuring and magic feature too in "Jelly Baby", when events get disastrously and horrifyingly out of hand at a children's party. This is a story calculated to make you want to leave the light on long after it should be off!

"The Chemical Man" hovers on the very thin dividing line between a ghost story and a tale of science fiction, but qualifies for inclusion here rather than in our sister collection *Space 2* (which I hope you will also read!) because of the revelations about the past which the mysterious drug reveals to our stately-home guide. And very disquieting they are too!

"The Shepherd's Dog" might make you weep a tear or two. Personally I find it hard to resist animal stories, especially stories about dogs, and this one, alone out of all the stories in this book, features a ghost who is not merely benevolent, but positively saintly! If you need an antidote to the horrors that will surround you elsewhere, this is probably it. I think the story is beautifully written by Joyce Marsh, who successfully avoids the pitfalls of excessive sentimentality.

You may remember Elizabeth Fancett's school story "Cassius" in *Spectre 1*. (If not, *read* it!) In her new one, "Ghosts Look Like People", you will find out how true that particular observation is. She again takes a school background, and weaves around it a highly ingenious adventure tale with an added twist on the very last page. It all goes to prove that the supernatural can be found in the unlikeliest places.

"The Judge's House", another story by Bram Stoker, the author of *Dracula* (after "Crooken Sands" in *Spectre 1*), is about the ghost of Judge Jeffries, the notorious "Hanging

Judge": this is the only story that you might have come across before. "The Tall Woman" describes a haunting which is all the more effective because the victim deserves all she gets. "A Matter of Timing" ends the book on a note which is perhaps the most disquieting of all, for it makes us ask certain fundamental questions about ourselves, and who we really are.

Lastly a word about the authors. Tim Stout, who has contributed two stories, is a very promising new writer whom I can guarantee that you will be meeting again in subsequent collections. His "Haunted Hollow" and "Jelly Baby" are sufficiently contrasted to stand up on their own merits. Chris Parr ("TA/9/73") is a TV playwright, and Frances Stephens ("The Chemical Man") is well known as a novelist. Joyce Marsh ("The Shepherd's Dog") has contributed to several short-story anthologies, and Pam Cleaver is a book reviewer and journalist as well as a writer of fiction. Rosemary Timperley is a prolific novelist and playwright, and has herself edited several ghost-story collections. Elizabeth Fancett, whom I mentioned before, and the only contributor making a return visit, has contributed to many other anthologies, and is to be found also in *Space 1*. Gladys Greenaway ("A Matter of Timing") is also a novelist.

I want to thank them all, and I do hope that you enjoy reading *Spectre 2* as much as I've enjoyed compiling it.

Don't forget to let us know what sort of stories you enjoy best. It will make our job in choosing *Spectre 3* that much easier.

Richard Davis

The Hand from Haunted Hollow
Tim Stout

He was miles from anywhere when it happened.

A series of thuds shook the old blue Morris and the temperature-gauge needle, which had been fluttering frantically for the past ten miles, shuddered and swung past the red. Clouds of steam gushed from under the bonnet to eddy against the windscreen.

Although twenty years spent dinning the Classics into the thick heads of obstreperous schoolboys had implanted a powerful self-control in Leonard Ferris, he allowed his exasperation full rein and subjected the hissing car to a blistering verbal lashing as he steered it into the nearest lay-by.

Savernake Forest: what a place to run dry! Trees filed away endlessly to all points of the compass, and he'd seen very little traffic since leaving the motorway half an hour before. Pointless checking the boot for an emergency top-up supply; he was one of those people whose cars ran on optimism. If he wanted a refill he'd have to strike off into the woods where with luck there would be a stream and, with a

11

bit more, some sort of container. Leaving the car simmering he jumped the parched roadside ditch and threaded his way into the maze of trees.

At least it was a nice day. His normal good spirits returned. After the strain of getting his pupils through their end-of-term examinations it was a relief to be turning his back on the College for the holidays.

Savernake was surely one of the oldest English forests. The tall, ancient timber had probably seen out several centuries and very likely the spongy leafmould underfoot had dampened the ankles of Civil War soldiers just as it was dampening his. He stooped to tuck his trouser bottoms safely inside his long fawn socks.

A stream would be on low ground; maybe below the promising green slope a little way ahead. He had not gone far when his ears caught the tinkle of water. He stepped forward cheerfully. The quest seemed to be over almost before it had begun.

The stream was little more than a dribble over moss and pebbles, but perhaps lower down it ran deeper. Ferris followed its erratic course further and further into the forest. Though he kept his eyes open for empty bottles or other litter that might serve to carry water he noticed not so much as a sweet wrapper. Didn't trippers ever come this way?

Going back to the car and flagging down the first car that came along began to seem the wisest course, but Ferris was strangely reluctant to forsake the will-o'-the-wisp trickle with its glinting half-promise of deeper water just out of sight. Imperceptibly, his pursuit became a descent until he reached a steep bank where the stream flowed under a thicket to sprinkle below as a miniature waterfall.

Lured on by the ageless spell of running water and heedless of the mud streaking his tweed suit, Ferris clambered down through the bushes until he came to level ground. He ducked out from beneath the branches, found himself in the open and blinked in astonishment at the unexpected view.

12

The enchanting little dell might have come from a fairy-tale picture-book. Sun danced across a clear, rippling lake and sparkled on the half-dozen rills splashing from between the encircling trees, while among the spreading lily pads red-billed moorhens bobbed and called. From the water's edge daffodils strayed over the hollow to the doorstep of a woodland cottage almost too good to be true.

Beneath a roof of shaggy grey thatch, leaded bottle-green windows winked at the sunbeams and tossed them onto the copper facings of a garden sun-dial and the polished handle of an old-fashioned pump. Had this delightful nook belonged to him, thought Ferris, he would never have wished to leave it.

Here at any rate was water in abundance, and surely the owner would not deny him the loan of a bucket. He went to the front door and gave a polite tap with the brass pixie knocker.

A minute later he was still waiting. Perhaps the householder was a warden or gamekeeper at present out in the forest. Ferris gave a couple of extra raps and was contemplating looking around for a bucket himself when the response came.

In the depths of the house something stirred and roused itself from rest. His ears caught the tread of heavy feet, not from a nearby bedroom or parlour but unaccountably approaching from a point beneath the ground. Ferris stood silent and perturbed while the footfalls shuffled to a halt a few yards from him on the other side of the door.

Nerving himself to announce his presence a third time, he was lifting the knocker uneasily when through the square of green glass above it he glimpsed the outline of a face peering out.

He thought better of disturbing the mysterious inhabitant further, turned and was hurrying away when the door creaked open behind him.

"You'll come back—won't you?"

A gentle entreaty was the last thing Ferris had expected,

but an apprehensive backward glance soon dispelled his vague feelings of unrest. From the cottage doorway a very old woman was beckoning him to return.

"Is there something you want, young man?"

He put her at ninety at least. Fine white hair drifted across a time-worn face as soft and pallid as a mushroom, but the eyes that met his from behind her octagonally-lensed spectacles were the crackling blue of a freezing, wind-whipped sky.

Despite her brown shawl and huge brooch of blazing topaz there was an indefinable chilliness about the old woman, and Ferris found himself entertaining the odd fancy that the sun was reluctant to get too close.

Yet there was nothing but friendliness in her smile as he explained his predicament.

"A bucket? Yes, I'm certain I can lay my hands on something. You'll come in, won't you?"

He stooped under the low lintel and followed her into a small, dark hall unlit by any window save for the barely translucent green glass. At once the old woman closed the door behind them, and for a moment of unreasoning panic Ferris feared he would be fallen upon and devoured. Instead she smiled at him again.

"I always keep everything shut, otherwise the sun gets in and dries things up so."

Ferris nodded, privately reflecting that a thorough drenching in sunlight and fresh air was just what was needed to banish the peculiar odour of damp, freshly-turned earth that was wrinkling his nostrils.

"If you'll wait here."

She threw him another bright, cold smile and disappeared down a shadowy passage. For some time he heard her heels tapping. Then they faded away as if she had descended to vaults deep underground. Obviously the place was far more extensive than he had thought. He looked around, but the gloom was almost impenetrable. How could anyone bear to

14

live in such murky surroundings? The installation of electricity in such an isolated dwelling might well be a difficult matter, but even so there were still such things as candles . . . As it was, the cottage, so attractive from without, was within little better than the lair of some wild beast.

He pulled open the door to have something to look at and daylight ventured a short way into the passage down which the woman had vanished. Ferris began to feel uneasy again—though cobwebs spanned the narrow walls and dangled from the ceiling, neither their unbroken patterns nor the dust coating the floor bore any trace of the comings and goings of the inhabitant. What manner of place was this, and who or what had he summoned forth? As Ferris went to investigate, a shadow fell across the mouth of the passageway, obscuring it.

"I shouldn't go down there, young man."

Somehow she had emerged from whatever gulf lay below the house and had returned by way of the front entrance. In her hand was a large bucket made from a hollowed log.

"Will this do, do you suppose?"

Ferris strove to behave as though nothing out of the ordinary had happened.

"That'll be fine," he said. "Just what I need."

The old crone seemed in no hurry to let him out of her cottage and remained in the doorway blocking his exit. Repeating his thanks, he reached out for the bucket and as she passed it over he saw that the middle finger of her left hand was missing. On the creased, half-healed stump quivered a droplet of blood.

The old woman saw him looking at it.

"That? Oh, I was careless with a saw. It was years ago now, but, it's such a funny thing, it never healed properly. Just imagine."

She grinned, put the hand to her shrivelled lips and slowly sucked the bleeding flesh.

"A saw?" Ferris repeated, trying to hide his distaste.

15

"That's what I said, young man—a saw. A jigsaw."

She cocked her head, inviting the obvious question.

"Were you making a jigsaw puzzle?" he asked, anxious to be done with her.

"I was, and I still do."

She nodded with such avidity that Ferris felt sure there was a hidden message. Perhaps if he complied she would get out of his way, let him fill up the bucket and go. He fumbled in his pocket.

"Do you make them for—er, sale?"

"Certainly not!" the old woman bridled.

Mentally Ferris cursed himself for saying the wrong thing.

"Making jigsaw puzzles is my very dear hobby," she snapped. "It's all I have left now—do you understand that, young man? All! I put something of myself into each one. They are all my sons and daughters. Mothers never sell their children, do they?"

"I'm terribly sorry. I only meant—"

"Would you like to see one?"

Again Ferris detected a hint of glee in the high-pitched, piping voice.

"You'd like to, wouldn't you? Eh?"

She moved closer and nudged him with a bony shoulder. What could he say but yes? He nodded and tried to look interested.

"I thought so! Open that cupboard by the door."

He did as ordered and found it stocked with over a score of square wooden boxes. He lifted one out. On its lid was a view of the whole dell, including the cottage. It was surprisingly well painted. Peeping inside, he saw the box was half-filled with the irregularly cut pieces of the puzzle.

The old woman took it from him.

"No more nonsense about buying and selling. This one is yours as a present from me."

She fingered the lid.

"All my puzzles show the same scene. I paint what I see,

16

and what I see is my home and the lovely forest. I hope it will remind my visitors to return and tell me how they enjoyed doing my jigsaws."

"I certainly shall," mumbled Ferris as he took the proffered gift. He shrank from touching the bright red spots that had dropped onto the lid from her still-oozing hand, but there was no help for it. As soon as he could without giving offence he furtively wiped his stained fingers against the rough wood of the bucket. But the old woman smiled and he knew she had noticed his discomfort.

"Now hurry up, draw your water and be off with you to your precious motor car," she said smartly. "Don't trouble yourself about the bucket. I have several others."

Stepping aside, she finally let him out into the sunlight. He turned to thank her.

"You've been most kind, and I shall look forward to doing your puzzle, Mrs . . . er—?"

"Not Mrs anything. Grandmother Green—you'll find it on the puzzle. I sign them all. Now be sure to look in on me next time you're travelling these parts."

"I shan't forget. Thanks again."

Ferris crossed to the pump, filled the bucket and looked round to wave goodbye to the old woman. There was no one in sight, but as he scrambled back the way he had come he thought he heard a cackle of laughter from the cottage. He looked once more at the idyllic scene. Nothing had changed. So why was he so glad to be going?

The hustle of the holidays quickly elbowed the old woman from the forefront of his mind. Ferris was a widower, but an enthusiastic member of local literary and photographic circles and a talented artist who made full use of the good sketching country around his hillside home. Not until an unexpected squall wrecked his ancient generator and robbed him of light for the evening did he think again of his breakdown in Savernake Forest.

Since the one oil lamp in the house was not bright enough to read by he decided to make the best of the situation by assembling the puzzle he had been given. He placed the spluttering old lamp beside him, dropped two cherry logs into the open grate and drew up a small table to his fireside armchair.

The scent of smouldering timber softened the lamp's hot fumes as Ferris propped up the painted lid in front of him and sifted the straight-edged pieces from the pile of coloured wooden fragments. A while later he had linked up the puzzle's rectangular border. It was larger than he had expected; quite a work of craftsmanship. He wondered how long it had taken its maker to create the woodland scene with her brush before painstakingly dissecting it with her jigsaw.

What did an actual jigsaw look like? Presumably, from what she had said, there was some kind of blade. A peculiar business that, her hand never healing up. A peculiar business all round. He bent over the table.

The next assortment of pieces all bore the shimmer of water. The lake, obviously. He set about attaching them to the frame of treetops and leafmould, but the more he pieced together the more the picture mystified him. Surely the lake had been fresh, sun-speckled and so clear he had glimpsed green weeds waving on the bottom? So his memory ran, and so it was shown on the lid of the box. The dismal stretch of dark water forming beneath his fingers was not at all what he remembered and the lake's far shore should have been obscured by the gentle spray of waterfalls, not sliding banks of dull, grey mist.

Perhaps the dim, yellow light and irritating oil fumes were to blame. He rubbed his eyes.

But the next few pieces only perplexed him further. No bright lilies, but rotting tree trunks and rank marsh sedges bordered the stagnant lake, and sharp-edged reeds transfixed the floating image of a bloated moon.

There seemed no reason why the puzzle should differ from

18

the scene on the box.

The old woman must have been even more eccentric than she had seemed.

Though he took up handfuls at random, each new piece fitted directly onto the completed portion of the puzzle, and the lake was soon finished. Ferris stared at the jigsaw with a baffled frown. Gone was the waterside pump at which he had filled the bucket. In its place loomed the misty silhouette of a derelict scaffold.

Ferris felt a stir of apprehension. He pondered over the abnormal circumstances in which the puzzle had come into his possession: first his unexpected discovery of the hollow and cottage, then the mysterious sounds from within, the woman's inexplicable passage through the intact cobwebs and lastly that horrible business of the severed finger and bleeding stump. Better perhaps to throw the confounded thing into the fire; he didn't much care to continue with it. He picked up the poker and cleared a space between the logs, but after a few moments of unsettled brooding decided to see out what could be only a poor practical joke.

Almost nothing in the puzzle corresponded either with his recollection or with the illustration on the lid. It was half finished before he began to be aware of the direction it was taking.

What was coming to life on the table before him was no idyllic glade but a macabre study of an abandoned burial ground.

In place of daffodils, tilting headstones heaved their lichen-scummed shoulders into the chill night air. Where he had looked for a picture-postcard cottage, a gaunt cold tomb rose like a deserted palace above the array of Death's grim standards. Yet something lived there, for through its shattered windows, obscured by pale hordes of circling moths, there glimmered a sickly green light.

The lamp's wick was burning low, but a sudden urge to see the full eeriness of the completed puzzle overrode Ferris's now redoubled feelings of aversion. His hands scrabbled amongst the pieces, which slid quickly into place as if from long practice.

Beside the lake stood four restless black horses harnessed to an old-fashioned hearse. For a wild moment he thought he saw their eyes roll and his heart bounded in alarm, but it was only the trick of the flickering light—of course it was. Why should he fear a mosaic of painted wood which he could tear asunder in a second? He wished he had the nerve to do it.

Shivering, he saw that the hearse had not come empty to the hollow.

Within the gates of the misty cemetery, four grey-bearded men in heavy black cloaks fought to restrain the wild struggles of a hooded figure clad in the garments of the grave. Ferris saw that the thrashing, shrouded body was strongly fettered with chains, and his gorge crawled with nausea. He could have sworn the jigsaw was writhing beneath his fumbling fingers.

As he reached up to wipe his sweating face, his tongue gagged in a cry of alarm. Something had smeared his hand with a trickle of fresh blood.

Several red droplets spotted the puzzle as he jerked his wrist in instinctive revulsion.

He hadn't cut himself; the skin was not even broken. It seemed that blood had simply burst from his veins. Ferris was now well and truly scared. He was alone in the remote house, his sole companion a failing oil lamp—or so he fervently hoped. There were only a few more pieces left. In a burst of determination to be done with the hellish puzzle once and for all he snatched up the remaining handful and stabbed them savagely into place.

In the forefront of the scene was the dark gulf of an uncovered grave. Now he could guess the reason for the prisoner's frantic efforts to wrench free, but it appeared the walking corpse was condemned to a death even more hideous than burial whilst still alive.

20

From the tomb issued a trail of huge, shapeless tracks. Piece by piece Ferris filled in the dwindling space and piece by piece the prints kept pace with him until, at the brink of the grave, they halted.

Aghast he heard the slow tramp of monstrous feet. He shuddered at the now all too familiar reek of dank earth that had first pressed itself upon him in that fearful cottage. Catching sight of his hands, he found that blood once more bedewed his fingers, and with a desperate cry flung himself from the table knocking the barely glimmering lamp to the floor.

As he groped for it, a tiny but blood-chilling shriek shrilled from the puzzle and on springing up he saw that it had dissolved into a scene more frightful yet.

The being in the shroud lay sprawled beside the grave, still chained but with the hood ripped from its shoulders. Around it stood the stern-faced quartet, one of whom now gripped a long, sharpened stake in black-gloved fists.

One piece remained. Hardly knowing what he did, Ferris took it in his dripping fingers and inserted it in the final gap above the captive's neck.

Blood spurted against the headstone as the executioner drove the stake through the bared throat of his pinioned victim. The terrified schoolmaster stumbled back, his scream of despair drowning the awful sounds from the graveside as he saw that the features of the slaughtered vampire and the name inscribed upon the monument were his own.

The old gallows creaked, and black ripples slithered over the lake in the midnight breeze now blowing hard against his pale cheek. The stench from the freshly dug grave rose stronger yet in his nostrils and unearthly footfalls thudded all around.

The familiar surroundings of his hearth faded. For Ferris, reality became the nightmare world of the jigsaw.

At last he found the courage to plunge his hands into the ghastly picture and shake it to pieces, but instead of the solid

21

table-top his fingers encountered cold, wet clay.

The cemetery's image buckled and crumbled, wrenched apart by something that was tearing its way up from within.

Out came a hand—a terrible, earth-stained hand red-flecked from the spatter of an oozing stump. A hand possessed of unearthly, supernatural strength.

It seized the fainting Ferris and silently carried him off into the depths below.

2 TA/9/73
Chris Parr

Things are going wrong today. Can't put my finger on it. I'm a fellow who likes his comforts and I've got my life pretty well organized. Living alone, I have my routine all to myself. A routine. That's important, don't you think?

My little flatlet—it's a nice place just off Goodge Street. I'm comfy here, don't have to share anything. Really comfy—that is, I suppose, until now. Well, routine makes me feel safe. I get up in the mornings, heat up the teapot, put two pieces of bread in the toaster and while all that waits, I warm up the porridge and make the tea.

I've got one of those shiny metal teapots—aluminium or something—you can see yourself looking funny in the reflection, know what I mean? So, I've got it all timed out nicely. Make the tea before the kettle steams up the little window, toast not too white or too brown, lashings of butter, then pour out the porridge into my blue dish. No time at all—got it all organized.

I make my porridge the night before, line up my plate, tea mug, dish, put the knife all ready, sticking into the butter, all ready for the morning. Makes me feel good to see it waiting for me every day, like someone else had done it for me.

Except this morning, there's something wrong.

Normally it's all there, right as ninepence, but today—I don't know . . .

There's a difference in the order. Things aren't in the proper place and—here—what's this? My knife is back in the cutlery drawer, with butter all over it and messing everything up. How could I have done that? Didn't put it there last night. Could have sworn. But it's not only that.

My porridge is salty.

I never eat salty porridge. I like it with two spoonfuls of sugar. Now that's another job I've got to do before work—put the porridge in the pedal bin and leave it ready to take down tonight. The bins in the area get littered with all sorts of rubbish this time of year, it being Christmas and all.

I've got a little stool I sit on to have my breakfast. It's a good stool. Comfy enough to relax on but not so comfy you want to stay too long. But there's something funny now—what's that reflected in the teapot? A movement, what?

Now I'm off that stool, quick as a flash and into the hall. Something was behind me there. But I see nothing, and this is the only way it could have gone. The hall is empty.

Here we are, with the last bite of toast. Looking at that teapot, it could have been the calendar fluttering near the door behind me. The window *is* open. But there's only December left on that calendar and it couldn't have moved like the way I saw that reflection . . .

Well, sitting here, what I think is—I saw nothing at all. But what I seem to think I might have seen was—scrubbing wire. That's the picture that comes to mind. Isn't that odd? Now you may laugh, but that's the truth as I sit here. You know—the sort of copper wire you scrub pans out with, the light glinting on it and all.

Can't think about that any longer. Got to get to work. I'm only one tube stop away from my job. I work for Mr

Burridge who owns the Joke Shop in Tottenham Court Road, near the tube. So I'm lucky. If it's fine, I walk. If not, then I tube it.

Not that my job's a joke, though. More like hard labour this time of year, what with the Santa Masks and false whiskers and all that malarkey. Got to check the invoices, select display items, store the rest and catalogue it all. I've got my own shorthand for that—like Santa Masks—that's SM followed by the code for the manufacturer, in this case no. 6, and then the year '73. Clever, eh? SM/6/73. Not bad.

Well, with this funny start to the morning, I've got to hurry. Late for work already. And now this coat. What's wrong with it? Get it off its hook in the hall—just a plain old blue duffle—served me well in the past. But what do I have here? There's a hole in the lining that wasn't there before, like a seam gone and I'm catching my fingers in it. Irritating. I tell you—workmanship these days. Just when you want to slip your arm in easily and get the thing on, it plays you up. There—what did I tell you? Got my blessed hand stuck. All right—let it rip. I'm in a hurry. Got to get into the street and down Tottenham Court Road. I'm four floors up. That's eighty-six steps. A lot at my age.

Oh Lord, it's nippy in the street this morning. Can see my breath. I have to huddle myself into this darn coat, hole and all. That really gets me, you know. Modern workmanship. You get it in the shop as well. Elastic that comes off masks, fizzing snakes that don't fizz, plastic ink puddles that break. Really gets me.

Take that Frankenstein Illusion Kit. Went a bomb last Christmas. Retailed at £4.50—a real winner. But what happens? A few go wrong and there I am in the shop with this geezer, an irritating carroty geezer who wants his money back. A bolt is missing. Well, it's not my fault, is it? Workmanship—that should be checked at the factory. I'm not on commission for what I sell. Passing trade is what I deal in.

So I told him to go and get lost. Don't bother me. See?

Know what? That fellow, he just wouldn't go. Stood there like he was cemented to the floor. Well, I've got three people queueing up with money in their hands for the Christmas Joke Tie. So what do I do? I get my old tool kit out from under the counter and shove him an old bolt from that. It doesn't fit, I mean, I know that, but I tell him to hop it, quick, like. So he goes.

Not that I'm hard, but I've got these customers waiting and I reckon he won't know the difference anyhow. Sensible. That's what I am. Maybe what Mr Burridge would call expedient, but I'm not one for big words.

Well, it's parky and I'm late and I have to make a decision. Really freezing, it is. But it'll be quicker to walk than take the tube this weather. Can't always depend on tubes, but Shanks's—well—I don't really go much on walking the length of Tottenham Court Road—don't like people—but walking is better than sitting in the tube on a winter day, with all that warm wet around you from the outside and glued next to some person who insists on pushing up to make three on the end of a seat intended for two. Know what? I never move up when they push. What I feel is—if they want to balance on the edge of that seat, nearly falling off—well, let them.

I'm half-way to work and there's frost in the air and there's this little stitch on my blue woolly glove that's gone. Something passed—quick as a whippet, snagged it and there—oho, here we go. A little run all up the back of my hand. Now, what was that all about? Did it snag? I bet not. Marching I might have been, striding a bit, with arms back and forwards. But that little ladder, bad workmanship—that's what. That's knitted goods for you.

The Christmas crowds are about. Even this early. The heads fair bob, they do, and there—oh, Lord, there it goes ahead of me, that funny copper glint. I think I see it, but it comes and goes and then—there you are. It's gone. There's a big fellow coming the other way and he blocks my sight. I get panicky. I sweat and it's freezing. Not myself, I can tell you.

Don't know why, but now I'm at the shop, I feel sort of safe. A silly panic I had. Well, I'm all right now. Jack's in first—he's got things sorted out upstairs. He can get on with all the Christmas stuff. Me—I'm taking it easy today. He can work this lunch hour. I'll be all right, just get my coat off and hung up. Funny about that seam . . .

This basement is cold. Makes me fair shiver. Well, I'm putting the heating up. Don't suppose Mr Burridge will like it. That's too bad.

I'm looking forward to my little treats. Know what I do? I celebrate every Christmas Eve. Not that I'm an indulgent man, don't go thinking that. But over Christmas, I have three days off, all quiet and on my own. Nothing much to do, see? So Christmas Eve I spoil myself. A little routine, like everything else.

What I do at lunchtime is go to the Fun Palace in Old Compton Street. I used to play the pinball machines, but now there's that new game they've got. I get my sandwich from the snack bar on the corner, then I play that funny electronic tennis game. It's really meant for two or four, but I prefer playing it by myself, my right hand against the left. Wouldn't want to play it with anyone else. I'm my own person and I like it that way. Nothing gets at me.

Now, I'm not a drinker, but on Christmas Eve I shut up shop smartish and nip down to the old Marquis in Cambridge Circus. Nice pub. Get four pints down me, spin them out until closing time. That's 72p altogether. Not bad for an evening out, but my lunchtime—now that costs me. Two quid I spend on that tennis game—adds up, you see, at 10p a go, but I have fun.

Mind you, for three quid I could get the Werewolf Special and scare the living daylights out of everybody. But working with the Nasties we have in the shop here, you get used to them—like the geezer who works in the sweet shop and never eats sweets.

But I do chuck the odd insect about.

You know—the Fly in the tea and the Metallic Cockroach on the floor next to some swanky bloke sitting peacefully in Lyons.

Tell you something. I taught myself a real lesson with that lark last Christmas Eve. Won't do that again. Too expensive. Almost ruined my Christmas Eve. Spoiled my treats.

Had this real special in. A Tarantula—big as your hand. Retailed at £2.25 and a bargain at the price. Code no. TA/9/73. No. 9 is for the firm it comes from—a place in North London. They make them really good—black rubber, eight thick legs, great fat body—but here's the crafty bit—real big black hairs all over it, set in the rubber, and tiny plastic hooks at the ends of the legs to give it a good grip. Beady eyes and a mean mouth. Really nasty.

Well, last Christmas I was saving the last one for the girl in the paper shop who always gets my change wrong. I put it in my pocket, ready for the morning. They open two hours Christmas morning for last-minute cards, bits and bobs, you know, and she would have been there for my little scare.

I'm looking forward to shutting shop and getting down to the Marquis when this same fellow—the one who grumbled about the Frankenstein Illusion Kit—he comes down into my basement. He puts that bolt I gave him down on the counter and demands a proper one or a new kit.

Can't repeat what I told him to do.

Well—it's Christmas and there'd been a rush and I was getting sick of customers. I ask you—five of them all wanting Magic Pyramids and we'd run out, so I sold two of them the Lose the Sixpence Coffin, except no one had a sixpence and 1p wouldn't work, and there was a fuss and they wouldn't take the Mummy's Hand instead because they said it was broken. Then this big woman came down wanting stocking fillers for her five-year-old and I told her we don't cater for toddlers or whatever you call them at that age, but she messes around with the showcases, so I sold her the Nail thro' Thumb and the Bloody Dagger. Retractable, of course.

And this fellow—he's still there. Wouldn't go. Not a big chap, not much bigger than me, so I could have bopped him one, but that's bad for business. Talk about a sticker. He just wouldn't go. So I'm rude to him and get the keys out, ready to lock up. And he still sticks. Glued to the basement floor. Never had trouble like that with anyone before—I'm a dab hand at getting rid of the awkward ones. But this one's a stubborn blighter.

He would *not* move.

Know what he said? Told me I was an unpleasant, mean little man. I ask you, *me*! So I tell him to shove off in no uncertain terms, and at last he begins to move. He's at the steps and he turns and he says he'll be back and I say, "Yes, mate, you do just that."

Then he's gone.

Well—here's the turn up—when I get to the Marquis there he is. Right in the middle of an office party, downing the Scotches, laughing and joking like he never knew how to get stroppy with anyone, and his arm around some typist in boots.

I don't like women. Never have. Bother and demands is what they're about and I can do without that.

So there he is, corners of his big mouth turned up, popular—all smiles and coppery curly hair, womanizing.

What do I do? I get mad—that's what. I put down my pint, I go up to the bar. I take old TA/9/73 out and drop it on his arm, casual like.

It clings. Really clings, like a live one. I think—I'll get better value out of this scene than wasting it on the girl in the paper shop, but do you know what that silly blighter does?

He runs screaming out of the pub right into the thick of the traffic in Cambridge Circus.

A real commotion there was outside then, with people darting in and out. You know, it took me ten minutes to get served—I ask you, service—yes—*ten* minutes I had to wait to get my money across the counter. But the thing that really made me mad was—that fellow never brought that tarantula back. He must've known it was me with my little joke, but he never came back in.

Wanted that back I did—could have had fun with it time and again. Well, at £2.25 you don't *give* them away, do you? Not even at Christmas.

I was thinking about that little incident a couple of weeks ago. Looked up the reference, then phoned to get some more. Know what they say?

"Sorry sir, discontinued line."

That's it, you see. Service.

Well, it's Christmas Eve again. I'm off. Jack can hold the fort this lunchtime.

This coat of mine has a life of its own, I swear. Like someone is holding it for me to put on, then nearly drops it to make me mad and—oho, here we go again. Fingers in the lining. This isn't my day.

Still parky outside. Christmas crowds thicker than ever. Too much money to spend, that's what I say. There's a mist in the air along Soho Square. Going to be foggy tonight.

I've got two quid silver in my pocket. That Fun Palace machine fair eats up the old coins.

Here we are, then. There's the tennis machine with my screen and the small dot zipping about like a slow bee. Now I concentrate. My 10p is in and here we go. Up come the bats—the little lines—length of your fingernail, one on each side of the line in the middle and the knobs below to make them move up and down and—here we go—this is living!

Bop. I hit the dot back and move the knob. I'm better with my right hand than my left. Bop. I get another one again, this time a crafty shot with the end of my bat and it shoots up to the top and down—there we go—zoom to the middle of my left bat then—bam—straight across the middle of the screen and bop—right up to the top again. I'm 3-1 to my right hand, but there's a shine on the screen and I can't see properly what's happening—what's that? There's a funny movement on the shine of the screen and no one to make it. Bleep—there, I missed one, and now another—this knob isn't turning right. And it's cold in here. I wish those blokes on the pinball machine would shut up, laughing like that. Do they have to have music on with everything here? Blaring noise. Can't concentrate.

Missed again. That little thing blipping away and my bat should have had it, except that this left-hand knob is working against me. It moves all wrong!

Here, this machine is dud—going to get my money back.

Must have a fag, quick—here—that's the left one back again. Now a light—come on, come on, my 10p is being wasted. There it goes, oh, come on—light up and get on with it.

Hey—what's *happening*?

This left-hand knob is doing something I can't control. It's winning. There's the dot coming back to me and—damn—there it goes, way below my bat, and here it comes again—here, this machine is *playing* me. It's sending the dot back as quick as it can.

This is crazy. The thing's mad.

The score is 11-3 to my left hand and my left hand has hardly touched the knob, what with my lighting up and all. Here we go—bop—12-3. I've lost. I mean, my right hand has lost.

Who is playing me?

I'm getting out of here.

It's parkier than ever and I can see a lot of my breath in front of me. Didn't stop to query that machine, but never mind. I've still got £1.90 change in my pocket, but Lord, it's heavy. How heavy.

It's heavy because I'm *running*.

It's really parky now, but I sweat again. Here comes Soho Square. It's coming fast. Come on, get back to the shop, you're safe there. Only a machine at that place—must have been something wrong. Forget the wasted 10p. Get that from the till. Mr Burridge won't notice.

There goes Soho Square, faster than ever, and the trees are disappearing into the mist. Can't see the tops. The light is fading. I'm really racing. I'm getting back to work. I'm safe there.

I'm in. Whew! That Jack makes a good cup of coffee. It's warm on my hands in the mug. Nice.

Only one customer down here in my basement. Let him browse.

It's gone quiet. The heating's down. Lighting's not so good either. Dim—positively dim. I tell you—these work-to-rules.

This man has a darkish coat on. He's bent over the display cabinet at the back. What I can see is his hunched up back and the trousers under the coat. All right, he can have a good gander at what we've got, let him make his mind up, give his order and out quick. I'm not messing about with advice. Not one of your Warren Street boys selling cars at fifteen hundred a go on commission. Just selling novelties on a straight wage, that's all. That's me.

This coffee's really good.

This fellow's taking a long time. Funny.

Here we go. He's straightening up. Now he'll come over, waste my time with questions, spend 50p and that's your lot.

What?

He's standing with his back to me and I swear there's a gap in the back of his head. Now that's silly. Must be a trick of the light. Light falls funny in this basement. Must be that.

He's very still. His hair on top is thick and reddish, a bit fuzzy in the light. But under his crown, right down to his neck is a—bloody—big—hole.

He's turning. What does he want? Oh, silly devil, he's wearing the Car Crash Mask. Come along then, come on.

He's standing, looking. Wants a mirror, I bet. They all like to see themselves in those masks, but half of them can't see 'cos the silly blighters can't get the eyeholes lined up with

32

their own eyes.

Bet he'll want some help.

Here—wait a bit. That mask isn't right. We had the nose bashed in and the eye drooped, but the jaw wasn't missing. The jaw was all there. This is—like—half a mask. Oh no. No jaw.

Now, come on, pull yourself together. What was the serial number of that mask? Come on—your own code. Look it up before he comes any nearer.

Here we are, CCM/4/69. What's this? No, it couldn't be—1969, out of stock. That's mad. I remember that mask clear as anything. They couldn't have discontinued it—or maybe I remembered an old one hanging around the place. But—

Now where's he gone? My God—just like that. Out in a flash. Bet he's nicked something.

There's something funny, though, lurking in the back of my mind. Oh—wait a moment—that's it. *Why was there no elastic holding that mask round the back of his head?*

Fair got out of there, didn't I? Left Jack to sort the shop out and walked myself stupid round Soho Square to calm down.

Well, I'm all right. I'm among people now. It's nice here in the Marquis. Got myself a pint and a seat, right away, didn't I? Not stupid. I know how to take care of myself.

Funny how that little incident at the shop upset me. What with everything else going wrong too. That was an odd geezer. Oh well, this is my little treat and an extra £1.90 to spend tonight. More than I reckoned on. Might stretch it to five pints. Won't quibble on that. And a new pair of gloves. That tennis machine did me a fair old favour.

It's nice and light in here. Plenty of people around. Christmas shoppers coming in, piled up with parcels and carriers. I've been watching them all—know them from the regulars. Good place this—bit of chatter, noise, people around me.

Think I'll order another one. What I'll do is put my gloves and the newspaper on my seat to keep it. If they get nicked, no one's gaining. Read the paper, gloves no use what with all the stitches gone. If they nick my seat I'll have them off it in no time. Can't lose.

Here we go. Bar's crowded. Always the same this time of year. Wonder if there'll be any office parties this Christmas? Bit of a giggle, watching them make fools of themselves, fellows thinking they can get off with the girls for a bit, then go home to their wives. Lipstick on collars. Silly fools.

Come on, woman. Can't you see I want to get served? Come *on*. If I bang my mug down, she'll get the message. Always the same, these women. You'd think they were blind. Well, I'll push along the bar a bit, get noticed.

That mirror's been there a long time, behind the bar. Proper old antique by now. They do say those mirrors fetch a fortune. Oh, come on—I'm next—

Oho—don't think because I've got my back to you, I can't see what you're doing. I can see your arm in the mirror pushing in through the crowd. You'll get a little gap, then in you'll be, quick as a whippet and get served before me. No chance, mate. I'm closing that gap—Lord—that funny wire. Copper wire.

Now I've dropped my mug. People are looking. Can't have that—no one looks at me like that. They're standing back. They look at me.

They can see this thing on my arm.

Get away—let me out. Let me by, *will you.*

This thing on my arm—big black hairy brute, jaws all ready to snap—poison me. Now, calm down. Think. Where are my gloves? If I can just get outside I can brush him off with my gloves.

No gloves. I'm out. It's cold. My bare hand will do—brush him off with my bare hand—that's it. The touch of the brute, hairs—he won't budge, he's got his eyes on me, he's staring at me. You'd think the cold outside would make him shrivel

34

and fall off.

But he gets fatter. He's staring and I'm breathless. He's the size of my bloody arm and he's coming for me.

I must run—I must—

Oh, God, the traffic . . .

3 The Chemical Man
Frances Stephens

John Lister stood looking out of the window, his back deliberately turned to the Great Hall. The place was getting on his nerves. Already the autumn afternoon was darkening, the gardens shrouded with rain, merging into the mist over the fields that lay beyond.

Not that he could see any of this very clearly. None of the windows at Merton Hall had ever been designed to open. The glass, product of some former age, was milky, distorted in places, so that even on the brightest day, rays of sunshine would be filtered down to an anaemic brownish-grey.

Lister shivered. The Preservation Society had spent vast amounts of money installing a central heating system in the ancient house, former home of the now extinct Bridgwater family, but there was a damp chilliness about this afternoon that defied any man-made invention.

A musty blanket of cold descended from the gallery, dust stirred in the gloomy cavern of a fireplace, while the sombre portraits gazed down like an alien species. What crank had ordained that, although the house had a power supply, there should be no electric light? Candles were considered to be more in character.

An oak door slammed, sending the noise reverberating far into the building. John Lister heard the sound of men's voices, the sharp crackle of laughter. Cheerfulness, like bright splinters, disintegrated the melancholy half-light. Lister recognized the everyday tones of his fellow guide and courier Charlie Anderson; the answering mumble of Eddy Sharp the caretaker.

Nothing got Charlie down. To him a job was just a job. As for Eddy, his mind was probably vacant whenever he started on his nightly stint of going over the vast area of floorboards with an electric polisher. How else could you put up with such soul-destroying boredom?

"It's gonna be dark if they don't get their skates on."

Charlie Anderson strode briskly forward, immediately bringing everything back into proper focus.

"And I particularly wanted to get away on time." Lister sounded peevish. "Four o'clock. They know our last tour is four o'clock."

He was glancing at his watch, calculating what corners could be cut when conducting his awaited party round.

"School crowd, isn't it? Sixth-form society. They'll know it all anyway."

Charlie's eyes were twinkling, for he enjoyed a bit of repartee, keeping one in front of the smart types. Lister wished he could still feel that way. Time was when the job had seemed a doddle—going through his spiel, selling a few postcards, coffee at all hours. Now . . .

A coach outside dispensed its occupants who were soon crowding into the stone-flagged entrance. Charlie, rubbing his hands, sorted them out, and Lister then started off with the first contingent. The words came automatically. He had said it all so often. They dawdled . . .

By the time Lister arrived home, there was no time to have a meal, only a quick shower before he presented himself for his evening appointment at the Medical Centre.

The doctor at the other side of the desk was white-coated and impersonal. After a few meaningless pleasantries, he fell silent, frowning at the papers in front of him.

"These reports—we have the full picture here. You're not married, I take it?"

Lister shook his head.

"And your age I see is—"

"Forty-one."

Cut the cackle, thought Lister impatiently. The doctor suddenly became brisk.

"The position is this. You have a very rare blood condition—almost a textbook case. There is no cure for this disease. Except—"

He placed his fingers in a pyramid, spacing them geometrically. Lister stared in appalled silence.

"Have you heard of chemical medicine? We have a new drug called Novatrax. A complete breakthrough."

The doctor paused.

"Novatrax will rectify your blood deficiency. But . . ."

But? Lister, scarcely comprehending the magnitude of these revelations, sat stone-faced, his eyes never leaving the man behind the desk.

The doctor searched carefully for words.

"This drug is decisive, but as yet too new for us to be fully aware of the possible side-effects."

"Side-effects?" asked Lister irritably. "What sort of side-effects?"

"I can't tell you. There may be none, and yet—"

Lister scraped back his chair, a harsh, nerve-splitting sound.

"So I have to choose between a blood disease and an unnamed threat. What kind of a choice is that?"

The doctor raised one hand slightly and let it fall.

"I'll need your permission for the treatment. Your

38

signature. A fortnightly injection of Novatrax . . ."

A paper was pushed across the desk. Lister signed, then rolled up his sleeve, as the doctor held up a needle to the light.

The next day was free. John Lister, out walking, made a determined effort to put the conversation out of his mind. A doctor, after all, was only a man like himself, liable to human error. See how the fellow had tried to safeguard himself, sharing out the responsibility of decision. Question: who was more involved, the man who bared his arm, or the one who pricked the skin?

Monday came. Lister returned reluctantly to work. Merton Hall had never felt less attractive. The gardens seemed dank and dead, while the air in the rooms had the smell and taste of age.

John Lister's resentment increased when the caretaker passed on a message that Charlie Anderson had 'flu and would not be coming in. More work for Lister. Nothing much scheduled this morning, but there were always casual stragglers. Later, a school party, then a women's organization.

Shoulders hunched, Lister killed time, waiting at the foot of the wide cantilever staircase, the only one of its type in the whole country. The baleful brass face of an eight-foot-high grandfather clock leered down at him from the first landing.

With their massively-carved balustrades, the stairs reached to the very top of the house, an opulent gesture on the part of architect and former owner. In other houses, such staircases run only to the first floor, servants and housekeepers reaching the upper storeys by means of narrow back stairs.

More and more Lister despised the house and the decadent way of life it stood for. The Bridgwater family, gazing down haughtily from their dark portraits, were drones and parasites. They had impregnated the whole fabric of the house

39

with their presence.

The school party consisted of ten-year-olds in the charge of a young woman teacher who did not have much control. Thankfully, she allowed Lister to take over. Tight-lipped, he surveyed the bobbing mass of heads, noting the jaws working up and down, the pockets stuffed with sweets. A paper packet dropped to the floor.

"I must ask you to be very careful," said Lister stiffly. "You are not to touch anything at all. As for litter—"

A tow-headed boy, standing alone, nonchalantly brought out a bar of chocolate. He screwed the wrapper into a ball. Lister fixed him with his eye.

The silly old fool. Think I'm going to take any notice of what he says? No chance.

Startled, Lister heard the words as though they had been spoken out loud. Yet the boy's lips were closed, his face open and ingenuous. In an overflow of innocence, he met Lister's glance.

"Could you tell us—that chair . . .?" the teacher murmured placatingly, covering up awkwardness.

Lister told them. The chair had been used by the hall porter in days of old. Carved of solid wood, it backed on to equally solid wall panelling. With a flick of the hand, Lister raised the catch, swung the chair forward, exposing a dark entry to a passage beyond.

Gasps came from the children.

I'd like to shut the silly old fool in there and lock the door.

The tow-headed rebel again. Lister's hand shot out to grab the little horror who, moments before, had been wedged within arm's reach. But the boy was no longer there. Apparently a loner, he was standing at the far end of the room, examining a display of postcards—too far away for even a penetrating childish voice to be heard so distinctly.

Mystified by this trick of sound, Lister started an abrupt commentary on the furnishings in the Great Hall. Impatiently he hurried the stragglers along as they milled in a ragged crowd. They asked the usual questions. Was there a ghost? A secret passage? He could scarcely tolerate their piping voices.

Feet clattered on bare boards as they passed from the Amber Bedroom to the Blue Bedroom. Lister paused on an enclosed landing, where a portrait of the Bridgwater family covered the entire wall.

"Here we see a portrait of Sir James with his daughters, Lady Mary and Lady Ann—"

He paused. Full daylight never reached this area, as in many parts of Merton Hall, but Lister had the uncanny sensation that the eyes in the picture followed him wherever he moved. Rubbish! Ancient oil and rotting canvas. And yet—

THEY don't like you either. They want to pay you out. If only I could—

Lister swung round in time to catch the tow-headed brat digging fiercely into the wooden wall panelling with a most unchildlike pocket knife. Already several inches of valuable oak were badly defaced. Grimly, Lister made the boy walk in front until the tour was concluded.

He always allowed a few minutes at the end for the purchase of souvenirs. Already the coach was waiting, but Lister took his time as the children surged outside. Almost casually he brushed the arm of the tow-headed child.

"Hang on a minute."

"What for?"

The boy scowled at him, hostile yet curious.

"Just something I think you'd like to see."

Lister's voice had the right amount of casualness in it, almost placatory, as though making amends.

Across the sweeping forecourt, he could see the school teacher in consultation with the coach driver. The Great Hall was empty.

"Over here."

Lister's fingers fastened decisively as he moved the boy,

41

now protesting and muttering, across the floor. The child, suspecting, started crying. Eyes glinting, Lister lifted the catch that secured the massive porter's chair and swung it forward, revealing the ominous dark beyond. A heave, and the boy was inside.

The catch dropped. It wouldn't matter now how much noise he made. No one would hear.

The school teacher waved as the coach pulled out.

Stupid woman, thought Lister contemptuously. Didn't she learn to count?

He felt curiously empty. His next party was easy. Women in serviceable hats and shoes anxious to be no trouble. He showed them round, carefully avoiding the porter's chair.

"You're not listening, are you? I expect you're tired. But I simply couldn't leave without . . ." The woman smiling at Lister had faded blue eyes and short grey hair.

"We *all* want to say thank you. *So* interesting."

The words had a far-away quality, dissolving into nothingness almost as they were spoken. Lister felt paper money in his hand.

He sought out Eddy Sharp, made an excuse, and left for home. That night he took pains to cook a special meal, eating slowly, and with great enjoyment. He slept well.

In the morning there was no sign of Charlie Anderson, but Eddy Sharp was hovering on the look-out.

"A fine mess-up here last night." Words, starting in a trickle, became a flood.

"That school party—some kid missing. You should have seen the cars. Parents and that teacher—it was *her* idea to move back the porter's chair."

"Go on," said Lister calmly.

"Kid of about ten. Yellow tee-shirt. He'd cried himself frantic—raving about being locked in."

Lister raised his eyebrows.

"I remember him—poking about behind my back. A real trouble-maker. He had only himself to blame."

42

"You think—?"

"Once that catch drops, how would anyone know?"

It was a quiet day. Eddy Sharp dealt garrulously with a reporter from the local paper. Lister went upstairs and left him to it. The brass face of the grandfather clock watched him malevolently. Tick-tock. Odd how he had never noticed the threat in that turgid sound before.

One of the first-floor rooms had an evil-looking display of knives and swords, reflecting the military prowess of the Bridgwater male line. Mindless butchers, thought Lister, despising them. This place, this hateful place, was nothing but a monument to greed and violence.

During the Civil War, the house had been under attack, and there had been hand-to-hand fighting on the stairs. Men cutting their fellow creatures down. And for what? Who would remember now?

When John Lister reported for his second injection of Novatrax, the doctor paused before he inserted the needle.

"Any reactions? Side-effects?"

"What, exactly?"

"Headaches? Black-outs, spells of dizziness?"

"No," said Lister carefully. "Nothing at all."

Days passed. It was extraordinary how well he felt. Indeed, renewed health made him impatient of other people's short-comings. Take Charlie Anderson, now back at Merton Hall, with his drooping shoulders and paunchy face. Did he have to turn up for work in a shirt with a frayed collar? And his eternal invitations. Come on round to our place, John. Drop in for coffee, any time. The wife'll be only too pleased . . .

The shambling nitwit. Did he think Lister had nothing better to do? It was a trial even to listen to his bleating voice. Hear him now. He must have been talking for the last ten minutes. John Lister had not registered a single word.

In the afternoon, he showed a mixed party round. The men, as usual, were only casually interested. Two elderly women made critical comments to each other, until at last John Lister was seething. Damn them, with their acid faces, their high and mighty manner.

The party came to the Long Gallery. Lister, struggling to keep his temper in check, stopped to explain how in bygone days the ladies of the Bridgwater family took exercise here when the weather made the paths too muddy for walking.

Who does he think he's talking to? A set of backward kids?

Even Lister, accustomed to muttered sneers, was stung by the supercilious tone. With eyes like needles, he stared at the vinegar face of the older woman. She met his gaze. Her tight little button mouth had not moved. And her friend was just finishing a yawn.

The tour proceeded. Even with his back to the two women, Lister could feel the force of their antipathy. It was inexplicable. He could feel the loathing. It twisted like maggots inside him, it scorched the skin along his spine. He was hurrying his party now.

I shall report this man to the Society. Everything about him is obnoxious. He should be removed from the job.

The words were clear and unmistakable. Yet Lister, glancing over a dozen or so faces, knew that no one else had heard. And the woman who had shaped the sentences had kept them in her head. But—

His head was swimming. Curtly, Lister cut off his monologue, shepherding his flock back to the starting point. He indicated the postcards and souvenirs.

Stupid, pompous prig! He'd be lost without a crowd to gawp at him. How I hate that type!

Wearily, Lister declined to look, for he knew the woman's face would reveal nothing. He went outside to stand in the open air.

It was a fine day, although cool, too cool for loitering in the grounds. The chestnut avenue leading to the house looked superlative against a sky that was the backcloth of approaching winter. Across the south lawn, a solid phalanx of hedges marked the substantial maze. Dry leaves skittered in the wind.

People drifted away, cars departed. The two old women were having their money's worth. At last they emerged. Lister, looking at the taller one, felt his stomach churn, detesting her long upper lip over horse-like teeth, the peppering of stubbly hairs. He masked his face with what he hoped was a friendly smile.

"Of course, the best view is from the south side. Quite unbeatable."

"Too late now, I think, and also too chilly." Horseface was drawing on her gloves.

"One disadvantage of a visit in the late season." Lister made his voice a tactful murmur. "You don't get full value for your entrance fee."

He had touched a valid point. The woman paused.

"Well—if we're brisk about it—mustn't miss the bus."

Lister walked steadily beside them, diverting their attention to the topiary and the ornamental fountains. One path only led to the maze, a quarter-of-a-mile labyrinth of eight-foot-high hedging. The smaller woman flashed him a questioning look, but Lister willed her not to defy him.

He felt the frost in the air as he returned alone to the house. *Get lost*, the horsefaced woman had hissed in her mind. She would have plenty of time to think about that now.

Lister sought out Charlie Anderson.

"It's Friday," he said, "and I haven't another party. Any objections if I get away now? I'd like to make it a long weekend."

Easy-going Charlie was prepared to co-operate. Lister went home, packed an overnight bag and caught a train to the country.

45

He had no trouble booking at a village inn, and he spent two solitary days striding the moors. His mind was curiously empty. No one knew where he was. If he wished, he need never return to Merton Hall. Yet some curious chemistry drew him back on Monday morning.

When he arrived, Anderson and Sharp were talking together. They glanced at each other as he approached, ill at ease, but then Anderson's face suffused with anger.

"Where've you been all weekend Lister? You stroll in here, cool as you like—I think we're entitled to some explanation."

"How is that?"

"How is that?" Anderson echoed the words, his voice hoarse with restrained fury. "Don't you know the mess you landed us in? You left two old women in that maze all night. One of them had a weak heart. She's in hospital now."

A small pulse of pleasure throbbed in Lister's forehead. Anderson lunged towards him, face blazing with fury.

"*We* took the blame, man! You haven't the remotest idea—"

In an upsurge of violence, he made to strike at Lister, but Eddy Sharp intervened.

"This won't help, although it upset *me* seeing those old women . . ."

He turned, walking away in the direction of the kitchen quarters. Anderson went upstairs. He had a favourite cubbyhole at the top of the house, where he always had the pretext of checking supplies of the thick, opaque candles that were used on occasions when dinners or parties were held.

Sharp returned with mugs of coffee. His weathered face was wrinkled with concern.

"What's the matter John? You can talk to me."

Absently Lister sipped his drink.

"Anderson will cool down, but you'll have to meet him part way," said Sharp.

"Sorry?"

Sharp stared hard into Lister's blank face.

"You've changed, Lister. I don't think you've heard a word I said."

On Friday, Lister reported for his injection of Novatrax. The doctor regarded him closely.

"Now if you have any worrying reactions, you are to get straight on the phone to me. Do you understand?"

Lister made himself concentrate. Normally the injection did not worry him, a mere prick, but this time it had given him the odd sensation of being entirely separated from everything and everyone else. The humming in his ears was building up and up, like the scream of some gigantic machine. He pulled on his jacket and hurried out of the surgery.

An early night would help him. Like a robot, he prepared for bed. He woke abruptly, having no idea how long he had slept, his mind raw with the instant impact of realization.

There had been no escape in dreams, for the creatures of nightmare were now his constant companions. In this moment of revelation, John Lister knew. Novatrax gave him life, but at what cost? By opening some door in the mind, he could identify only hate in others. He could pick out its very words. Kindness and love were silent.

He spent the day alone. Even to go out into the streets of the town seemed unwise. What would the warping of his personality lead to next?

The doctor had warned him that the effect of the drug was accumulative. There was no pain, only this heightened, almost terrifying sense of awareness.

Like a man drowning, something in Lister reached out to the person he used to be. Those had been good times with Anderson and Sharp. Before it was too late, he would make it right with Charlie Anderson. It was dark now, but there was a candle-light dinner at Merton Hall tonight. Perhaps he could catch Anderson before the guests arrived.

Rain was falling. Lister hastened through the darkness, hunched in his coat, shutting his mind to the alien sounds in the air, the howling of a dog across the fields, the shrill cries of children roaming the streets.

The great door creaked as he entered. Ye gods, the place *should* have been warm, but a sickly, damp chill met and enveloped him. Yet the table in the Great Hall looked attractive, with the warm mellow light of the candles.

The room was empty. Preparations made, extra staff would be supervising the arrangement of food in the kitchen.

Grey-faced, Lister heard the voices in the air, sibilant, whispering, growing louder—louder—only *these* were not people he knew. They were the distillation of all the hate and violence that had passed between these walls.

His eyes went up and up to the faces of the portraits, lips that were curved and cruel, eyes that narrowed with loathing, gloating on his helplessness. They had him now. A prisoner. He would never get away.

Paint on canvas. The words croaked in his mind, but he knew that he alone was the match that set them burning.

"Anderson?"

His own voice, a thread of a whisper. No one would hear. "Anderson, Anderson!"

Lister could not face a crowd of strangers in the kitchen. He heard a sound from above. Maybe Charlie was up there fussing about with the candles he kept in the cupboard.

The moment he mounted the first step, Lister could hear them all around him. Horrified, he realized that he was alone no longer, for the stairs were thronged with people, shouting, fighting, screaming. There was the clash of steel, the sickening impact of flesh against flesh, the obscenity of crunching bone as hands reached out for him, pulling, plucking, intent on destruction.

The smell of blood in his nostrils, he panted upwards.

The very woodwork was impregnated with palpable hatred. On the first landing, the yellow face of the clock leered and smirked. Towering dark and malevolent, the monster loomed over him. Now it was rocking forward—

48

nearer, nearer. It would crush him to pulp.

In blind terror, Lister dodged sideways as the giant came crashing down.

Gasping, he made the upper floor.

"Anderson, Anderson! If you don't hurry I—"

The air seared him with its blaze of evil. Now the dark wood panelling pressed towards him, to crush, to kill. There was nothing in the whole world but hate and vengeance, a wall of blackness running red with blood.

"Lister!"

The call reached him. Lister groped for the balustrade, peering down at the upturned faces, many feet below. The shocked countenance of Charlie Anderson clicked like an instant photograph in his mind, but it was too late, for nothing could save him now. Demons sang in his mind, the air rushed past him as he crashed down, down.

A silent group gathered by the broken body of John Lister.

The pathologist straightened up, wiping his hands as he spoke to the police officer.

"Blood normal, heart better than many men his age. No debts, no family conflicts. Then why?"

Lister could have told him. Who could live in a world where the only force of communication was hate?

4 Jelly Baby
Tim Stout

It was going to be a birthday to remember.

"I'll be ten," Valerie Reynolds told her schoolfriends proudly. "That's double figures, so I'm having a proper grown-up party."

Her father had arranged a special treat.

"Summon the Great Mephisto for an evening of thrills and enchantment. All the arts of the mystic Orient in your own parlour. Kiddie shows a speciality."

Prompted by the advertisement, Dr Ian Reynolds had dialled the number printed in the local paper and received the Great Mephisto's personal promise of a display of dazzling magic for Valerie's big day.

To his annoyance, on the evening of the party he was held up for two hours at the hospital when a young engineer was stretchered in with severe oxy-acetylene burns. Dusk was settling as, collar turned up against a sudden downpour, he hurried across the puddled car-park and scrambled into his powerful white Rover.

He'd agreed to be back by six. Valerie's party must have

50

started long ago, but at least it was only a short drive to his converted farmhouse. Glancing more often at his watch than at the speedometer, he cut through the empty country lanes and was rounding a blind corner fast when his full beam threw up a minivan parked dead ahead.

Bloody fool, slung right across the road without a light showing! Reynolds slammed on brakes but though he wrenched to the right his rear nearside caught the smaller vehicle a hefty clout. The minivan cannoned forward several feet. A cry from the rainy darkness was cut short by a splash from the ditch.

Reynolds jumped out.

"Hello there! Anybody hurt?"

He stared in surprise as his powerful motoring torch lit up the side of the mini.

Painted in fluorescent green letters six inches high was the slogan "The Great Mephisto—Prince of Magic". Beside the dented vehicle, as if conjured up by one of his own spells, glowered a peppery little man whose bedraggled dinner jacket and satanic black beard dripped duckweed and ditchwater upon the road.

"For heaven's sake why don't you watch your speed?" he snarled.

"I beg your pardon!" Reynolds snapped back. "Where are your lights?"

"Lights? You try having them without a battery. I was fixing the damned thing when you came hammering into me."

He scowled at the back of his minivan.

"Charming! Miles from anywhere, wheel-arch stove in and I was on my way to a job. You're a right one, aren't you, chummy?"

Reynolds introduced himself. It was the Great Mephisto's turn to be taken aback. Some of his belligerence evaporated.

"Let me give you a hand with your things," Reynolds suggested. "You can clean up at my place before the show."

51

Mephisto shook his head indignantly.

"You've got a hope. The show's off."

"Oh, for goodness' sake. It was an accident. What do you mean, off?"

The fiery little man waved his fist in Reynolds' face.

"I can't perform, that's what! Blame yourself. You've sprained my wrist with your rotten driving."

Reynolds frowned. "Can you suggest anyone else? If you're thinking of your fee, I'll see that you don't lose by it."

"Oh . . . well." Mephisto reflected. "It's no good though. Conjuring is a bit of a closed shop, see. I reckon I'm about the only one in town."

"Look," Reynolds appealed. "I've got God knows how many children waiting at home for somebody to turn up and give them a conjuring show. Now come on—surely you know a few others?"

Mephisto thought it over.

"There is another place," he finally admitted. "But I wouldn't be doing you a favour. Moving about, you get to hear things . . ."

"Complaints? Is that what you're saying?"

"No. More the other way around."

Reynolds shrugged. "Your professional jealousies aren't my affair. How do I contact them?"

"One of these comes through my letterbox every month."

Mephisto handed over the card as if glad to be getting rid of it. Reynolds examined the square of stiff black celluloid. A telephone number was stamped on one side. On the other, letters shimmered across the dark reflective surface.

"For the night of your life", they read. There was nothing else.

He slipped the card into his pocket.

"I'm obliged. Won't you let me give you a lift? You can call a garage from my home."

The Great Mephisto shook his head.

"Not if you're ringing that number. I don't want to be within a hundred miles of your place tonight."

"Suit yourself."

Reynolds gave the conjuror his insurance company's address and drove off. What was the matter with the fellow? He seemed almost paranoid about other conjurors.

At the first telephone box he dialled the number on the card. The exchange code was unfamiliar, and the line was very bad.

He bellowed his request. It was like speaking to Australia.

"Can you help me? I want your top man—I've been let down at short notice over a children's conjuring show."

The receptionist's far-off voice barely reached his straining ear.

"It's very busy tonight. There's no one here except the Director."

"Well, what the devil am I to do?" Reynolds bawled into the mouthpiece. "I must have a conjuror! What about this Director of yours—will he come?"

There was a burst of static that sounded like a cackle of laughter. Then he caught the receptionist's faint reply.

"The Director has agreed to visit you. Please give me the details."

By the time Reynolds got home the party was in full swing. Valerie ran down the path, kissed him and planted an orange paper hat on his head.

"Thank goodness you're back," sighed his wife Teresa. "There are about thirty of them inside playing a game with the cushions."

She pointed to a fruit-juice stain on her blue trouser-suit. "The mess! The noise!"

Reynolds went to his bedroom and put on slacks and a cardigan. When he reappeared on the landing there was a motionless grey figure waiting in the hall below.

As he came downstairs the man turned to face him. Reynolds found himself gazing at a tall, imposing stranger with a great leonine head and a mane of glossy grey hair.

"Dr Reynolds, no doubt?" The visitor's blue eyes twinkled from wrinkled pouches. "I hope I'm in time."

"You're the—er—conjuror? The Director?"

"Indeed I am." He inclined his head in a courtly gesture. "You asked for my services, I think."

Reynolds hid his surprise at his visitor's sudden materialization.

"I'm most relieved to see you. It's a filthy night. I'm sorry nobody heard you arrive."

He helped the Director off with his raincoat and waited for him to remove the close-fitting gloves that matched his dove-grey lounge suit. But the stranger made no move to take them off and after an awkward pause Reynolds indicated the staircase.

"Yes—well, you'll want to get ready."

He showed him into the bedroom, then left him to prepare for the show. Not until he reached the hall coat-stand did he realize that despite the rain the mackintosh over his arm was bone-dry: nor could he recall seeing a trace of dampness on the Director's flowing hair. He opened the door—there was no car outside. How then had his strange visitor escaped a soaking?

The chaos in the lounge took some quelling. With Teresa's help Reynolds corralled his daughter and her boisterous young friends in one end of the long room, and was still trying to settle them on the carpet when he heard a step on the stairs.

He went into the hall. The conjuror carried no props and was still dressed in his grey suit and gloves.

"I'd thought you'd be in some sort of costume," Reynolds queried.

"I am," came the reply.

Reynolds couldn't help thinking it was a strange thing to say. Instead he continued: "Forgive me for not asking your name before. How shall I introduce you?"

54

The conjuror smiled. "In my business it helps not to say who I really am."

"A touch of mystery? I understand. But we must think up something appropriate for the children."

The two went into the lounge and Reynolds led his guest to a small table placed before the chattering audience.

"Boys and girls!" he announced. "May I present, straight from far Baghdad, the astounding—the incredible—the truly astonishing—er . . . Uncle Marvel!"

With a dramatic flourish, he stepped aside.

The big man moved quietly forward and perched on the edge of the table, swinging his long legs.

"Hello. How nice to meet you all," he said easily.

Reynolds and his wife edged down the room and found seats behind the children, who were waiting eagerly for the magic to begin.

"I ought to start by saying 'Happy birthday'," said Uncle Marvel. "Where are you, Valerie?"

The little girl jumped up. With her brown curls and green dress she was a pretty figure.

"There you are! Well, Valerie, I've a confession to make. When your daddy told me you were ten today I bought some sweets as a present but on the way here I got hungry and—well . . ."

He drew an empty bag from his pocket and gazed at it in embarrassment.

"I'm afraid I ate them. I really am very ashamed of myself."

The children laughed as he hung his head.

"Never mind though! What about a spot of birthday magic to put matters right? Which sweets do you like best, Valerie?"

"Lime surprises," Valerie giggled.

"And very nice too. Lime surprises it is."

He held out the crumpled bag on the flat of his palm. Everyone in the room watched intently as it slowly filled out,

55

apparently crammed full by an invisible hand. Uncle Marvel waited until the round green sweets were bursting forth, then handed them over to Valerie.

"Many happy returns. Perhaps you'll take a few and pass the rest round."

As the bag circulated, Reynolds touched his wife's arm.

"This fellow's going to be good."

Teresa nodded. "Don't you think it's funny that he knew her favourite sweets, though?"

Soon the lounge was filled with the murmur of satisfied sucking. Uncle Marvel rubbed his hands briskly.

"Right! Let's get on with some real magic."

His narrow, vivid blue eyes wandered over his audience.

"Tony, down there in the corner! My X-ray vision tells me you have a pencil in your pocket. May I borrow it?"

How could he possibly have known the boy's name? Teresa asked herself.

"Thank you. Now, none of us has ever met before, but this perfectly ordinary lead pencil is going to tell me something about each one of you. Of course, it's not quite so ordinary now because I've just put a spell on it.

"Pens and paper for everybody, Valerie? Fine. You must all write down one question—and whatever you ask, this magic pencil of Tony's will tell me the answer."

There was much furtive peeking and crossing out as the children scribbled away. Then Valerie handed their slips of paper to Uncle Marvel, who put them face down on the table beside him.

"Right—the first question is from Danny, who bets me I can't tell you the name of his pet rabbit."

The conjuror looked up with a smile.

"Fair enough, Danny; let's see. I copy out your question, using the magic pencil—then the pencil takes over, and I just keep hold of it while it writes the answer."

There was absolute silence as, seemingly of its own volition, the youngster's half-chewed stub skimmed across the paper with the conjuror's fingers resting lightly upon it. Uncle Marvel glanced down.

"His name is—Pippin, and he's black. Fair enough, Danny?"

The little boy beamed with pleasure as his friends cheered the magician.

"Mine next!"

"Read mine now, Uncle Marvel!"

Amid the clamour Reynolds grinned at his wife.

"He's way above what I expected. How do you think he pulled that off?"

Uncle Marvel wrote an answer on each child's paper. Most had kept to their families, school and each other, but Valerie's question startled her parents.

"Why was Daddy late?" she had written.

"He was treating a man whose arms were hurt in a factory fire," was the response. "He will recover the use of one, but the other will be amputated."

Reynolds was thunderstruck. "He must be a mind reader!" he exclaimed to Teresa. "How else could he have known? He's absolutely right: the welding torch caught the poor chap on the elbow."

Uncle Marvel handed the slips back.

"What about a game of Air Raid? Everyone make a paper dart. Boys, will you show the girls how? That's the idea."

At his bidding, the children cast their darts into the air together.

The ensuing aerobatics were out of this world.

Instead of a short, simple glide the darts dived, climbed, looped the loop and flitted above and below each other like aerial fish in a great aquarium. Seconds passed and none dropped to the ground.

"Boys, you're manning anti-aircraft guns!" cried Uncle Marvel. "Clap your hands each time you fire. Girls, you're the pilots—try to fly between the batteries."

There was pandemonium as one by one the darts suddenly

lost the power to stay aloft, staggered and fell to the carpet. At last only Valerie's dart was still airborne, hovering inexplicably beneath the lounge light.

"Come on, boys! Bring her down!" Uncle Marvel shouted. He had sprung to his feet, his head thrown back and his seamed features alight with a fierce pleasure.

"We'll get her together."

The fingers of both his gloved hands blurred in a clicking fusillade. Both children and adults exclaimed in astonishment as the little girl's dart caught fire and spiralled down from the ceiling. Uncle Marvel clawed it out of the air and savagely crushed the burning paper in his fist.

Reynolds could scarcely believe his eyes.

"How does he do it? How can he?"

"Haven't you realized? He isn't!" Teresa Reynolds' voice was sharp with worry. "The children are: he's done something to them. And did you see the way he looked just now? Something's wrong, Ian. This isn't just a children's party any longer."

But there was no doubt about the reaction of the children themselves. Uncle Marvel had them eating out of his hand.

A minute later Teresa was called upon to fetch a bucket of water for the goldfish that each boy and girl found in their glasses of lemonade. Out in the kitchen, she dipped in her hand. They were all real enough.

Then came the tortoise Uncle Marvel brought to life from a picture gummed on a paper hat. They all saw it plod forth from the coloured tissue before the magician turned it into a glass model "to get him out of the way".

Teresa's alarm was fast hardening into fear.

"What if something happens to one of those children?" she asked her husband.

"Darling, I can't just jump up and order the man out," Reynolds muttered. "Besides, nothing can possibly happen. This is the treat we promised Valerie, remember?"

A telephone rang.

"Excuse me."

Uncle Marvel reached inside his jacket and took out a small red hand-set. He listened, said something Reynolds didn't catch and replaced the telephone.

"Sorry about that—it was my pet dragon Gobbles, wondering why I haven't been home to get his tea. He really is just the greediest dragon."

He shrugged ruefully.

"So I said—and I hope you'll all feel I did the right thing—well, I'm busy giving a show to some very nice young ladies and gentlemen, so why not come along and have one as a snack while you're waiting?"

Teresa clutched Reynolds' arm.

"Ian—look at his face!"

Uncle Marvel's lips crawled apart in a hungry smile. There was a hot light in his crinkling eyes.

"So he's on his way." He paused. "But I'm forgetting—I don't suppose any of you believes in dragons any more, do you?"

"No!" the children roared happily.

"Quite right too; of course not. Just remember that and Gobbles won't be able to lay a fang on you. He's got about sixty, by the way. Would you like to see for yourselves?"

The children were bursting for a glimpse of the non-existent dragon.

"Yes!" they chorused.

"Splendid!" Uncle Marvel bestowed an avuncular smile upon them. "Gobbles will be so flattered. We'll have him in, then, shall we? Valerie, would you take up that rug by the window?"

Teresa's knuckles were white on her husband's trouser-leg.

"There's nothing there but bare boards," he reassured her.

Valerie pulled back the rug and gasped in surprise. Let into the wooden floor was a hinged trapdoor.

"Can you hear him?"

Uncle Marvel motioned the children to silence.

"He's clawing his way up from down below."

Teresa bit back a scream. Her straining ears caught a muffled snorting and the scrape of a lumbering body.

Green smoke began to waft through the trapdoor hinges. Slowly the flap lifted.

Uncle Marvel squatted down and peered inside.

"There you are! Come along, Gobbles. The boys and girls are all here waiting for you."

The green smoke thickened, and a throaty snarl issued from the depths. The startled youngsters scrambled back.

Teresa's heart pounded. There really was something down there under the house; something huge and horrible that was going to leap out amongst the children.

"Stop!" She jumped up, hands clenched tight.

Uncle Marvel lifted his head courteously and smiled into her eyes.

"It's tea-time," she gabbled. "You've delighted us enough for the moment. Perhaps in a little while—"

The conjuror rose to his feet. "Of course. Stupid of me—I hadn't noticed how time was passing. Be off with you, Gobbles. I'll be home shortly."

He pushed back the trapdoor with his foot and slid the rug across it.

"Well, children, you've had a lucky escape. Gobbles has a big appetite. But it seems tea's ready now and I'm sure your appetites are even bigger."

He stepped aside as they dashed to the laden table. While Teresa busied herself with paper plates and cups, Reynolds approached him with the offer of a drink.

"A first-rate performance. You certainly know some extraordinary tricks."

"How kind of you, Dr Reynolds." Was there a hint of mockery in the tall man's courteous bow?

"Just a few stunts for the youngsters. It keeps me in practice."

"Practice?"

"I don't always perform in front of children."

Behind his smiling eyes, the shutters were down as tight as a coffin lid.

"I'm sure you don't." Reynolds sensed his abrupt coldness and fumbled for the right words. "My wife and I were wondering . . . er, we'd prefer you not to continue in quite the same vein. Some of Valerie's friends are a little impressionable, you understand. We don't want them upset."

Uncle Marvel's glassy level stare was not making it easy.

"So soft-pedal it a bit after tea, could you? Rabbits out of a hat—that kind of thing."

The magician glanced at the children around the table.

"Do they share your views, I wonder?" he murmured.

Reynolds answered with some asperity.

"They don't have to. The fact that they are my views is sufficient. You will please do as I say."

Uncle Marvel shook his head.

"I won't, you know."

He made a small movement with the thumb and forefinger of his left hand. Reynolds vanished into empty air.

From the corner of her eye Teresa saw him disappear. She left the tea-table and struck the gin and lime from Uncle Marvel's gloved hand.

"What have you done to my husband?"

"Just a little magic. I thought it might amuse the children."

"Bring him back this minute or I'll have the police round here!"

"You insist on being reunited?"

"Yes. Now!"

Uncle Marvel reflected. "It might be better. As you say: now."

His fingers quivered a second time, and the next instant he was alone in the lounge with the children. They were waiting at the table, gazing eagerly at the jelly and trifle. He strolled over.

Valerie looked up. "Where are Mummy and Daddy?"

Uncle Marvel patted her shoulder.

"Not far off. They had to slip away for a moment, and asked me to cut the cake instead."

He stretched across the table and tweaked off the colourful cake cloth. There were oohs and aahs from the boys and girls.

It was a confectioner's masterpiece—a magnificent palace of meringue and icing-sugar set upon a hillside of green marzipan.

"Exquisite," said Uncle Marvel admiringly. "Who made it?"

"My mummy," Valerie told him proudly. "It belongs to a fairy queen. Isn't she clever?"

"Extremely clever. I live in a castle too, you know. Would you and your friends be interested in seeing it?"

They all nodded enthusiastically.

"Very well. I'll try to make it appear. Be sure not to look, now."

The children sat waiting, eyes obediently closed.

"All right. Here it is."

The hand of corruption had passed over the fairytale cake. Its battlements were crumbling into grey dust, and delicate bluish mould spider-webbed up the blotched walls. The hill had gone. In its place beneath the grim fortress lay a cemetery of dark jelly dotted with headstones cut from shelled almonds.

The children were silent. Then a small boy peered forward and said doubtfully, "Look! There's somebody down there."

Uncle Marvel glanced over his shoulder.

"So there is. Sometimes a magician can surprise even himself."

Reynolds was not a particularly fit man. Squirming loose from the purple world in which he had awoken entombed was draining his strength.

62

Blackcurrant: it was a flavour he had always disliked. The pungent fumes clogged his throat as he kicked, flailed and bit his way free from the sweet, sticky pit. He struggled up, fighting for balance as the quivering muck shifted underfoot.

Nearby, a curved slab of what looked like old ivory emerged from the dim purple depths below. He steadied himself against it and looked around.

Memory and recognition rushed back in a flood of despair. He was a shrunken, helpless manikin, trapped in an expanse of reeking jelly. The smooth white nut he gripped had nearly proved an edible marble monument to his living grave.

He lifted his head. Above the cemetery reared the ramparts of the terrible castle and higher still, like encircling mountain peaks, were the faces of his daughter and her friends.

"Help me! Valerie—help me!" he shouted.

Why did they continue to laugh and point at him?

"Hello, Daddy!" Valerie called back in a voice like a rumbling goods train. "You look just like a jelly baby—and you sound like a little mouse squeaking."

He gasped. The girl had taken his miniature appearance for another of Marvel's party tricks, and his voice was now so high-pitched that shouting to her was useless. A trick! He knew now that nothing he and Teresa had witnessed had been a trick. What manner of place had his telephone call reached? What kind of visitor had he welcomed into his home?

Suddenly he became aware of choking nearby. He turned, and uttered a cry of grief.

Surrounding the cemetery were ten tapering columns of pallid wax, tall as war memorials—Valerie's birthday candles. Strung up on the closest, gagged and chained to the towering pillar, was his wife.

"Darling! I'm coming!"

Her head twisted round, her eyes wide with terror. He could see her mouth struggle against the gag.

Why couldn't he move faster? The jelly was a foul

blackcurrant quicksand that slurped and tugged at his feet as he stumbled on between the jagged, fang-like gravestones.

"Teresa!" he called. "I'll get you down, I swear!"

Thunder hammered the upper air. Uncle Marvel was chuckling. Instinctively Reynolds covered his head. Then he looked up.

The magician's face was a stormcloud of grinning frightfulness hanging low over the castle. He peeled off his gloves and flexed two huge, scaly hands.

Green smoke drifted from the gigantic fingers that came groping into the graveyard and hovered above the tiny figure shuddering on the candle. Fire flashed from the pointed talons, igniting the wick. The fettered woman writhed like a trapped animal as molten wax dripped down towards her upturned face.

Though Reynolds' futile screams of fury and despair hardly carried beyond the castle courtyard, the watching giant seemed to understand him.

"Come, Dr Reynolds, you insisted on having the best," he said reprovingly. " 'I want your top man'—remember?"

Reynolds dropped on all fours and scrabbled across the jelly as fast as he could, praying that he could rescue Teresa before the candle flame set her long, blond hair alight.

"A pity you didn't trouble to inquire our terms. Took them for granted, perhaps? Throughout history, I've never tried to hide that my services come high."

A polished cake knife appeared in his hand.

"However, I've taken a liking to you, Doctor."

A jab from the point sent Reynolds sprawling face-down in the jelly. The smell of blackcurrant was blotted out by a sudden sulphurous stench.

"I shall have to insist on claiming your body, of course. It won't take more than a moment. Rather a nasty moment for you, I'm afraid.

"But as for your immortal soul—well, just this once, I'm prepared to forget it."

The glittering blade sliced down.

5 The Shepherd's Dog
Joyce Marsh

Chauval lifted his head sharply; his sensitive, upstanding ears twitched as he listened intently. From outside the window a little twig scraped against the pane and the big white dog recognized it as the sound which had roused him from his uneasy sleep. His body relaxed as he allowed his shaggy head to drop down onto his forepaws.

He did not sleep again, however, as his olive-green eyes, lightly flecked with little pin-points of golden light, stared fixedly at the still form on the bed. For two long days he had watched that figure, waiting to see the tiniest movement of life, although by now his every sense told him that he hoped in vain.

On that morning when the Master had not risen as he usually did at first light of day, Chauval had been impatient and slightly irritable. Even through the closed window his sensitive nose had picked up the exhilarating scent of the new day. His limbs almost ached in their eagerness for that glorious, rushing scamper over the heather with which every morning began.

65

Restlessly he had padded around the room, scratched at the closed door and lifted his head to savour the fresh clean smell of a new day. Then a long deep growl had begun low in his throat, but still the Master had not moved. The growl had become a whine, anxiety replaced impatience and Chauval had crept closer to the bed. He had thrust his nose beneath the Master's shoulder and nudged him violently. The man's head rolled on the pillow, but he had not opened his eyes nor made a sound. One still hand dangled from the bed; Chauval licked it—it was so cold.

Then the big, shaggy white dog had jumped onto the bed, covering the man with his body, licking at his face and hands as he tried to drive out that dreadful cold with the warmth of his own body.

It was then that the vague anxiety had become a sickening fear, for the Master's well known scent had gone and in its place was a smell that Chauval knew and dreaded.

So many times in his long working life the sheepdog had found a sheep which had wandered too near the edge and had fallen to its death on the rocky beach below, or a straying lamb which had become stranded on a ledge to die of fear and hunger. All these animals had the smell of death on them and now that same hateful scent was upon the Master.

Chauval, in his panic, had leapt from the bed and rushed first to the door and then to the window, his head lifted in a long despairing wail. Instinctively he knew that with his great strength and size he could, if he chose, break out of the room, but without direct orders from the Master, he dared not try.

All his life, ever since he had first come as a tiny puppy to the lonely cliff-top cottage, the Master had ordered and directed his every action. It was the Master who had taught him how to guard sheep, it was he who had told the dog what to do and when to do it. Even in those carefree, happy moments when work was done and the shepherd's dog was at liberty to rush pell-mell over the springy turf and wind-

66

scorched heather, Chauval never forgot the law of instant obedience, for his playtime began on the Master's command and ended with his whistling call.

Chauval had been happy and secure in his trusting devotion, but now the Master's voice was still and the dog was alone and desolate. In his bewilderment and confusion there was only one thing of which he could be certain. When he was alone his duty was to stay on guard, so for two long days and nights he had been in his room. Even the gnawing hunger and thirst was forgotten as he crouched low, every muscle of his body tense and alert to protect his Master and his home.

Suddenly Chauval's head lifted again as another, much louder noise came from outside and the draught, blowing in through a broken pane, carried the scent of a human. Silently, but with his lip lifted in the beginnings of a snarl, Chauval moved to the window and raised himself on hind legs to look out.

On the path, a few yards from the cottage, stood a man. His head was thrown back as he shouted loudly.

"Are ye in there, Will? Are ye all right then, Will?"

Chauval looked back quickly towards the bed, half hoping that the sound of a voice might have called the Master back to life; but still there was no movement from the bed.

The dark-haired man, still calling the Master's name, had come very close to the cottage and was rapping on the door with his heavy stick. Chauval's snarl became more menacing and the hairs on his back stood up stiffly. He knew that man and he knew that stick. Once, a very long time ago, he had felt its weight upon his back; the man had come into the cottage whilst Chauval was alone and had walked into rooms and looked into places where only the Master was allowed to go. The dog had barked once in warning and the man had hit him with the stick. Now that man was an enemy—never to be allowed inside.

The knocking on the door had ceased as the man walked

67

around the cottage looking in at all the windows. He came to Chauval's window and stopped to peer inside. For a brief moment the man and the dog stared into each other's eyes. The sound of the dog's angry barking echoed in the room and the man leapt back in startled fear.

But he realized that he was protected by the glass between them and he came forward again to look past the frantic dog into the room. He stared in for a moment and then, turning quickly, he ran off. Chauval fell silent. In the distance he could hear the soft, melancholy bleating of the sheep and further away still, the wild rushing of the sea hurling itself against the barren rocky beach.

Stiffly he dropped down from the window and crept back to resume his vigil by the bed, but weakened by lack of food and little sleep, the spate of barking had exhausted him and his eyes closed again in slumber.

A long time must have passed for the room was almost dark when Chauval was once more roused by the sound of footsteps and loud voices.

There was a violent banging on the cottage door and Chauval heard it fly open with a crash. Swiftly he leapt onto the bed, crouching over the defenceless Master. He was sweating with fear and the perspiration ran off his tongue to hang in wet, sticky streams from his mouth.

The voices came nearer and nearer; the bedroom door flew open and in the opening was the man with the stick. The huge white dog remained motionless, hunched protectively and tense above his Master's body. His lip curled upward, showing long, yellow teeth and the whites of his eyes gleamed through the dusk.

"The great ugly brute will ne'er let us come near. We'll have to shoot him first."

It was that harsh rough voice of the man with the stick. Chauval gathered himself to spring, but suddenly someone else spoke, softly and gently.

"Poor thing, he must have been locked in here for days, he's

68

half starved. Maybe I can coax him out."

The cruel voice muttered and mumbled but the man stood aside and his place in the doorway was taken by a stranger.

"Good dog, come on then, we'll not hurt you, good boy, that's a good dog."

The stranger's voice was kind and reassuring. He held out the back of his hand with the fingers hanging limply down.

"Good dog, come here then."

With infinite slowness Chauval eased himself off the bed. Never taking his eyes from the stranger's face the dog crawled slowly across the floor. With all his heart he wanted to trust this man.

"For heaven's sake get on wi' it. We haven't got all night to mess around wi' yon vicious brute."

The harsh voice spat out the words and out of the corner of his eye Chauval saw the stick raised above him. With a powerful spring he leapt up and his teeth fastened on the hand holding the stick. He felt the warm taste of blood in his mouth as his body thudded into the man's chest and bore him backwards to the floor.

The room was full of noise and the smell of human fear. The stranger's voice, no longer gentle, was raised above the other's and his was the hand which snatched up the stick and brought it down hard on the dog's back. With a yelp of pain and anger Chauval turned to snarl a brief defiance at the stranger who was now another enemy, and then he sprang past the men towards the open door. Frantic hands grabbed at his long fur, but snapping and snarling the dog pulled himself free and leapt outside. With a few bounding strides he reached the cover of the bushes and threw himself down in the tangled bracken.

In an agony of confusion and fear he stared at the cottage. He wanted to go back inside to continue his guard over the Master but he dared not. Lights had sprung up in the windows and the sound of voices drifted out. The front door stood open and suddenly two men came out carrying something wrapped in white. Instinctively Chauval knew that it was the Master.

The man with the stick had brought the stranger and Chauval had been driven out. They had forced him to abandon his post and now his enemies were taking the Master away. The big dog raised himself up onto his haunches, his green eyes glittered in the twilight darkness, and he began to whimper softly. Then he flung back his head, the long snout pointing directly upwards towards the pale moon and the whimper became a long howl of desolation and despair.

"There he is, over there! Shoot him, someone, while ye've got the chance. He'll be no good now old Will's gone and if he turns rogue he'll be a menace to all of us."

It was the harsh, cruel voice, and close upon the words came a sharp crack and a singing bullet passed close to the dog's ear.

Chauval began to run as he had never run in his life before. Leaping, bounding, with lolling tongue and eyes bulging until they were nearly bursting from the sockets, he crashed through the bracken and undergrowth.

The lights in the cottage receded to pin-points and the shouts of the men were borne away on the night breeze, and still Chauval ran. The scrubby trees and bushes thinned and the ground beneath his feet became more sharp and rocky as he fled up the steep craggy hill which rose sharply from the cliff-top pasture. At last he could run no more and he flung himself down onto a flat rock.

His sides heaved and the breath rasped in his throat. The pounding of his heart quietened at last and he breathed more easily, but now he was tormented by thirst.

The big dog raised his head and the sensitive nostrils quivered as he explored the night wind for the longed-for scent of water. His senses told him that water was not far away, but he did not immediately go to find it. Instead he peered anxiously down the slope and listened intently. In his headlong flight he had taken no care to hide his trail and his enemies could easily track him down.

To his relief he could hear only the sound of rushing wind; for the moment he was safe. Gleaming wraith-like in the darkness the dog weaved a cautious zig-zagging course towards the water. The clear mountain stream flowed abundantly. Bursting out from a fissure in the rock, it cascaded first into a deep pool before it ran off down the hillside. Chauval thrust his muzzle into the icy water and greedily drank his fill.

He was ravenously hungry but the wild, rushing escape up the steep hill had drained the last of his strength and he was too exhausted to search for food. A flat, jutting shelf of rock offered him some shelter and he crept beneath it. Wearily he buried his nose into the long warm hairs on his flank and slept.

Chauval awoke at the first light of day and at once felt the gnawing, agonizing hunger. He had never in his life needed to find his own food; no one had ever taught him how and now he had no idea where to begin. He whimpered and whined, calling for the Master. Even now he could still desperately hope to hear a whistle or the beloved voice calling his name, but all was silent except for the tinkling water and the lonely singing of the wind.

His green eyes flicked restlessly as he surveyed the barren hillside—there was no food here. There would be food in the cottage if only he dared to go to find it. Hunger overcame fear at last and moving carefully with his body close to the ground he crept down the hill.

The cottage was deserted, the strangers had gone and the Master had not returned. In the pale light of dawn the dog moved around the house, scratching at the closed doors, but there was no way to get in. The sheep, left unguarded, had strayed into the tangled undergrowth near the cottage, where they bleated dismally. Instinctively Chauval moved around them, expertly gathering them into a little flock and herding them back to the grazing land. Enviously he watched them

71

eat their fill of the succulent grass.

Suddenly he heard the sound of a sheep in distress and behind a large rock he found a young ewe with her lamb stretched out on the ground beside her. It had fallen from the top of the rock and its fleece was streaked with blood. The mother bleated pathetically, but the lamb was quite dead. With an expert little rush, Chauval drove the ewe away and nudged the lamb with his nose. It was still warm and the sickly sweet smell of the fresh blood made the juices flow in his mouth; but it was forbidden to eat the flesh of a dead sheep and Chauval would not disobey the Master's law—he would die first.

"Good dog, you may eat the lamb."

The well-known voice sounded loud and clear in his ear. With a little yelp of joyful surprise Chauval looked round. The breeze blew in off the sea and the sheep called softly to each other, but there was neither scent nor sight of the Master and yet his voice came again urgently.

"Eat, Chauval—eat or you will die."

The pangs of desperate hunger gnawed agonizingly at his insides, but there was no need now to hesitate. Somehow and from somewhere far off the Master had spoken.

The long yellow teeth ripped and tore at the soft flesh as, with ravenous haste, the dog wolfed down the fresh meat. So intent was he upon satisfying his hunger that he did not immediately notice that he was no longer alone on the cliff-top. A man, a woman and their son were running towards him. They were shouting and waving their arms and Chauval heard them at last and looked up from his meal. He gave a quick welcoming bark; he knew them and they were his friends. Suddenly the youth bent down and picked up something from the ground and the next moment a sharp, hard rock flew through the air to hit the dog a stinging blow on the head. He yelped in pain and surprise; there was no doubting now the menace in their voices and gestures. Suddenly and inexplicably even these friends had become his

72

enemies. Once more he fled upwards to safety. The full and satisfying meal had restored his strength and he moved swiftly.

The people stood by the bloody remnants of the lamb and watched him go.

"That were Will's old dog," the boy said.

"Ay, an' I should 'a had my gun handy. He'll have to be shot now, he's turned sheep killer."

The woman answered her husband and there was pity in her voice. "Poor thing, 'twill be a mercy to put him down or like as not he'll starve to death, for he'll not let us near him, that's for sure."

And so the barren rocky hill became Chauval's home and refuge. Water he had in abundance but food was a constant nagging problem. Once or twice he managed to catch a young rabbit, but mostly he lived by what he could scrounge or steal from the scattered cottages on the cliff-top. He always had to take care to search for his food when the people were asleep, for at the very sight of him they drove him off with sticks and stones and even guns.

At night or in the light of early dawn he slunk down the hill, moving cautiously with his body close to the ground. The Master's voice had never come again to give him leave, so he would not touch the sheep. In the pale light he moved like a great white shadow through the flock and they, knowing him to be their friend, never ceased their constant nibbling at the grass as he passed.

While the cottagers slept he padded silently around their homes, sniffing and searching for the scraps they had thrown away. Sometimes he ate the foul-smelling mash which the good wives had put out for their chickens. At other times he found a clutch of eggs laid in the undergrowth by a straying hen. Once in his maraudings he was attacked by a little, half-wild cat; he had killed it and in his desperation had eaten even that.

In the weeks since the Master had gone the sheepdog had

73

grown thin and gaunt. His long coat, wetted by the rain and dried by the sun and salt breezes, was filthy and matted. Twigs, thorns and brambles had become entangled in the long hairs where they fretted and scratched his skin when he lay down.

At night, especially when the moon rode high in the heavens, he yearned so desperately for the Master that he lifted his snout to the stars and let forth a long, desolate howl. Below, in the little hamlet, the people would hear his mournful wail and shudder in their warm cosy beds.

One morning he had been particularly unsuccessful in his search for food; the sun had risen and the cottagers were stirring, yet his ravenous hunger would not allow him to abandon his scavenging. Suddenly he heard a door opening nearby and in a quick, panicky scamper, he made for a clump of bracken where he pressed his body close to the ground and trembled.

The cheerful sound of a woman's voice drifted out through the open door and a few minutes later, a tiny child, tottering on unsteady legs, came out into the garden. Chauval pressed down even further into the concealing bracken and his heart thudded painfully. The little boy was coming closer and the dog dared not move, for he could not escape without being seen.

With the casual curiosity of the very young the child was peering into the bushes. Suddenly he saw the white dog and his eyes flung wide in surprise. For a moment he swayed uncertainly on chubby little legs and then plumped down in front of Chauval.

"Hello, doggy," he lisped, "do you want thum buppy?"

With trusting friendliness he offered a thick crust of bread liberally spread with butter. Chauval took the food gently in his front teeth and wolfed it down. The boy gurgled his pleasure and stretched out his little hand to scratch and tickle at the sensitive spot behind the dog's ears. It was so long since Chauval had felt a loving, friendly touch, and his delight

74

in it now made him forget even his hunger. He crept forward and rested his head on the child's lap.

"Does doggy want thum more buppy?"

The little boy scrambled clumsily to his feet.

"Come on doggy, let's get more buppy."

He set off towards his home encouraging his new friend to follow. Longing to feel again that loving, friendly touch, Chauval crawled out of his hiding place. With tail tucked between his legs and head hanging low he slunk after the boy, but his progress was slow and the child grew impatient.

"Come on, silly doggy."

He grasped the dog's ears in both his little hands and tugged with all his strength. In an excess of grateful affection Chauval reached up and licked the baby's face, and it was at that moment that a piercing shriek rang out from the cottage doorway. A woman's voice shouted urgently.

"Husband, come quickly, the killer dog's got our Ian."

Chauval leapt sideways and the child, startled by the note of fear in his mother's voice, ran to hide himself in her skirts. The woman was thrust aside and her place in the doorway was taken by a man—it was the man with the stick, only now it was not a stick but a gun that he held in his hand.

The terrified dog raced for the concealing cover of the undergrowth, but he was too late. The shot sounded almost in his ear and the searing bullet ran along his side, gouging a deep, bloody weal in its path.

For a moment or two Chauval ran on and felt no pain, but after a while his limbs stiffened and every thudding step was an agony. He knew he could never reach the safety of his rocky retreat and he veered off towards the only other hiding place he knew—the tall rock on the cliff, behind which he had found and eaten the lamb.

He reached the rock and crept gratefully into its concealing shadow, pressing himself as close as he could to the cool hardness.

The bullet wound was painful and for a long while he

diligently licked at it until his rough tongue had cleaned it and soothed the pain. Weakened by the lack of food, the effort exhausted him and he fell into a deep sleep.

When he awoke the sun had long since reached its peak and had begun on its slow slide down towards the sea. Chauval was thirsty, his nose felt hot and dry and the inside of his mouth burned feverishly. He longed for the cool waters of his mountain stream and he peered cautiously out of his hiding place. The sound of human voices drifted over to him and the dog drew back in alarm.

Not far away, across the rich green pasture, a man, a woman and several children were playing with a ball. They laughed and shouted in their play but their gaiety brought neither comfort nor reassurance to Chauval. He knew that he had but to show himself and their happy voices would become rough and harsh as they came at him with their sticks and their guns.

Behind him the cliff dropped down sheer to the sea; there was no escape that way and the only way to safety was barred by the group on the cliff-top.

Patiently the big white dog settled down to wait his opportunity to slip past his enemies. As he watched, one of the children wandered away from the group and, unnoticed by the others, came towards Chauval and the cliff edge.

The breeze carried his scent to the dog's sensitive nose and he recognized the tiny boy who had befriended him that morning. The child tottered to the very edge; with all the strength in his fat little arms he threw a pebble out over the cliff and chuckled as it rattled and clattered onto the beach below.

So many times Chauval had seen the Master's sheep venture too near to the crumbling edge of the cliff—he knew what should be done. Like the sheep, this human child should be herded back to safety, and yet if he were to venture out, he would be seen and the man would attack.

The boy swayed out dangerously on the very edge and

76

Chauval could not decide what to do. In his anxiety he whimpered softly.

As he watched the child with an ever-increasing confusion there came upon him an icy chill; he began to tremble violently. A small misty cloud had drifted in from the sea, enveloping him in its clammy touch. The hairs on his neck bristled and then, from somewhere in the vapour which hung over him, came the voice he had so longed to hear.

"Chauval, my good Chauval," it called, "go then, boy, fetch him back."

There was no hesitation now. The Master had spoken and Chauval leapt to obey.

"Steady boy, easy now," the voice called from behind, and the good sheepdog lay down in the grass. Then quietly, so as not to startle the child, he moved forward in a series of little rushes. As soon as he was able the dog placed himself between the boy and the cliff edge. The child, unafraid, lunged towards him gurgling his pleasure; but with a warning snarl Chauval forced him back. Again the child came on and this time the dog herded him away from the edge with a little nip on the fatty part of his leg. More startled than hurt, the boy gave a loud indignant wail and ran at his protector with his clenched fists—but again Chauval urged him backwards from the cliffs.

The man and the woman had heard their son's cry and were hurrying to his rescue. Chauval paid them no heed as, with all the skill he had learned from guarding sheep, he forced the child to safety. It was the man who reached the child first and snatched him up in his arms.

"Get away, you evil brute."

He lashed out with his heavy boot. Chauval leapt back but the blow caught him full in the chest, forcing him nearer to the edge. The man aimed yet another vicious kick and the dog felt his back legs slip away into space. The weight of his body dragged down and he clawed frantically at the soft turf with his front feet. For a brief moment he hung suspended,

77

but his grip was too tenuous and he fell.

Tumbling and twisting, Chauval hurtled down. The sea-gulls got up from their rocky perches and their shrieks mingled with the screams of the doomed dog. His body smashed down onto the rocks and earth; sea and sky were blotted out in one final stab of pain.

The blood-streaked flanks heaved once, twice, and were still. The birds settled back on the rocky ledges and from above the man and the women looked down on the still shape so far below them.

"Well, that's the last trouble we'll get from that vicious dog," the man said with cruel satisfaction.

"Aye," said his wife, "an' it might have been our Ian lyin' doon there. We've only the dog to thank that it isn't."

The man looked askance.

"You're a fool, husband," she went on, "you've seen a dog work sheep often enough. Could ye no see that it weren't attacking our boy, he were herdin' him back from the edge just like he would sheep."

The man hung his head. "Well, he's gone wild, he's better off this way anyhow," he said sulkily.

"Aye," she said, and they moved off while the child in his father's arms whined, "Nice doggy, where's 'at nice doggy gone?"

All was now very quiet upon the beach. The sun had dipped its rim into the sea and the shadows grew long and dark. A shrill whistle sounded in the breeze and a dark mist at the water's edge trembled like the heat haze of high summer. The misty cloud steadied and darkened and took shape. The whistle came again and a soft, white vapour hung over the body of the dead dog.

The cloud by the water's edge took on the shape of a man and he stretched forth his hand.

"Chauval."

The name was a soft sigh on the sea breeze. A great shaggy dog bounded forward, leaving behind the dead, blood-stained

78

thing on the rocks.

The man moved off over the sands and the dog by his side leapt and danced in a transport of delight.

Few people now will venture down onto that part of the beach; for it is said that, in the late afternoon, just as the sun is about to slide into the sea, a man and his dog walk the sands. Those who have seen them say that the dog's olive-green eyes forever glow with a loving devotion while the man smiles his contentment and as they pass, the air turns cold and is filled with soft sounds. Even the little waves breaking on the shore sing out the name: "Chauval, Chauval . . ."

6 Ghosts Look Like People
Elizabeth Fancett

"All right," said Big Sir. "Discussion time. Have you formed your groups, chosen your subjects?"

"Yes, sir," they chorused.

"Off you go, then—into the grounds. Keep a good distance between each group, record everything, and *discuss*—don't argue! I want a debate, not a débâcle."

"What's a débâcle?" asked Derry.

"Well, it's—oh never mind! Out with you all!"

"Ghosts!" scoffed Wigmore. "Puff and stoppycock!"

"He means stuff and poppycock," guffawed Drew.

"Stop talking like your father, Wiggy!" said Derry.

"It *is* a lot of nonsense," retorted Wiggy. "And not just because my dad says so. Ghosts are nothings—therefore they can't exist."

"I don't know," said David thoughtfully. "Lots of things exist that you can't actually see."

"Like the wind," said Derry.

"But you can feel it," put in Drew.

"And you can see it," added Derry. "At least, you can see what it does."

"Like mussing up your hair," sniggered Wiggy. "It looks a mess." He chuckled nastily. "But then—perhaps that's its natural state, seeing there *is* no wind today!"

"My granny says—" began Dooley, speaking for the first time.

"Who cares what your scraggy old granny says!" snarled Wiggy. "You're a nothing!"

"I'm *not*," protested Dooley. "I'm a—" He stopped suddenly.

"Well, go on—what *are* you?" egged Wiggy.

"Can it, man!" said Drew. "You're a pain in the neck!"

"Oh, stuff your silly old ghosts!" shouted Wiggy. He got up and walked angrily away.

"Good riddance," said Drew. "Now perhaps we can get on."

"I wonder what ghosts *really* look like?" Derry said thoughtfully.

Drew suddenly chuckled. "Man, I'd like to see old Wiggy's face if he met up with a ghostie! Say—couldn't we pretend—"

"No, we couldn't," said David hastily.

"Scaring people's silly," said Derry.

"Wiggy isn't people," said Drew. "He's—well, he's— Wiggy!"

"Let's stick to the point," said David desperately. "And I think that ghosts look like people; except—I believe—they don't cast shadows, you can't see them in a mirror and they don't eat."

"I can understand why they don't eat," said Derry. "They don't need to. But why don't they cast shadows or reflect in mirrors?"

"Because," said David, "there's no substance to them. It only appears so to us."

"Weird!" gasped Derry. She shivered. "Perhaps we've sat next to one—in a park, or the cinema. Ghosts like the dark, don't they?"

"Not always," said David. "If ghosts look like people, they move among people in the daytime—in shops, factories, at school . . ."

"Say," chuckled Drew, "supposing Big Sir is one!"

The three Ds collapsed into gusts of laughter, during which David hastily switched off the tape.

"I'll have to cut *that* bit out," he said ruefully.

"Why?" asked Drew. "Big Sir can take a joke. Switch on, son! Let's get this over with. I can hear ice cream bells in the distance."

David switched on again.

"*I'm* a ghost," said Dooley suddenly.

"Look, Dooley," said David kindly, "we can't include remarks like that you know."

"Why not?" demanded Dooley. "That's the subject, isn't it?"

"Bet you're glad you're *not*," said Derry. "Ghosts can't gollop ice cream by the gallon!"

"I don't eat gallons of ice cream," said Dooley crossly. "I don't eat any—only *pretend* to."

"Oh yes?" grinned Drew.

"I do! I do! Anyway, you never notice me, so you couldn't say what I do or don't do."

They shifted uncomfortably, and did not look at each other. It was a truth that hurt. Dooley was a bit of a nonentity. He was a duffer at most lessons and was plainly out of his element everywhere. They didn't mean to be unkind but—well—he just wasn't *worth* noticing.

And that, thought Derry, busy with her own conscience, was why he'd said he was a ghost. She knew a little bit about psychology. Some people would say anything, do anything, just to get attention.

She spoke gently.

"Seriously, though, Dooley. Do *you* believe in ghosts?"

"I told you," said Dooley. "I'm a ghost myself."

"Oh sure," said Drew. "If I pushed you, my hand would go right through you." He gave Dooley a gentle shove. Dooley fell over backwards.

"You're no ghost, old son! You can't get out of maths that way."

"I hate maths," said Dooley, righting himself. "Anyway, a ghost shouldn't have to learn anything."

"So why do you bother?" asked Drew.

"Because my gran says that even a ghost should be well educated."

"Anyone else got any point to raise?" cut in David.

"Can't think of anything," said Derry.

"Drew?"

"Except that there's no such things as ghosts." Drew grinned. "Or if there are—we don't believe in 'em!"

Seeing that Dooley was about to speak again, David hastily switched off.

"I believe in ghosts," said Dooley stubbornly. "*I'm* a ghost, and I can prove it."

"How?" asked Derry.

"By not being here."

"But you *are* here, silly!"

"Well, I'm not now," said Dooley. "Look!"

But they did not hear him, busy collecting their belongings.

"Hey," said David, "what's Wiggy up to now?"

They looked away at Wiggy who was obviously annoying another group.

"Forget the creep!" said Drew. "Let's go get ice creams!"

"Where's Dooley gone?" asked Derry.

"Home to lunch I expect," said David.

"From which he won't return," said Drew. "It's maths afterwards."

"It's odd, you know," said David suddenly. "He speaks of his granny as though she is still alive."

"Not odd," said Derry. "He talks that way because he

wants her to be."

"Must be rotten," reflected David, "to lose someone close."

"He's got his uncle," said Drew.

"A right, mean man," said Derry.

"You've been seeing too many pantomimes, my silly old sis," said Drew. "Wicked uncles don't exist."

"Wicked uncles *always* exist!" retorted Derry.

A burst of shouting interrupted their arguing. They saw Wiggy hurrying away from the group he'd joined. Suddenly he stumbled, fell face-downward.

"Illustrating a point, do you think?" asked Drew.

Wiggy scrambled up, turned back towards the group.

"Which one was it?" he demanded, glaring at their astonished faces. "I'll kill him, that's what I'll do, I'll kill him!"

"Clear off!" they yelled in chorus.

Wiggy began a hasty retreat, then he pulled up short, fell violently backwards into a yelling heap upon the grass.

"What's got into him?" asked Drew.

Wiggy was on his feet now, looking wildly about him.

"Hey, Wiggy!" called Drew. "Tumbling over your own trotters now?"

Wiggy started to come towards them.

"Did you see anyone push me?" he demanded.

"Well, old sport," said Drew, "I wasn't going to tell you this, but you bumped into a force-field the second time. I'm still working on the first shove, but I have it on good authority from Captain Kirk of the *Enterprise*, no less—that on an alien planet like this—"

"Did either of you see who it was?" demanded Wiggy of Derry and Drew.

They shook their heads.

"Didn't anyone see *anyone*?" asked Wiggy.

"Oh come on!" said Derry impatiently. "We've just time for an ice cream before lunch."

"I don't think I want any," groaned Drew. "The thought of that maths mock puts me right off."

"Who you kidding?" scoffed David. "Come on, race you both!"

"There's Dooley," said Drew, still running. "Thought he wouldn't be missing for long with old man Icy in the vicinity."

"What's vicinity mean?" asked Derry, puffing along behind him.

"I'll explain later," panted Drew. "Let's get there before Dooley wolfs the lot."

"Stop a minute!" gasped Derry. "I can't keep pace."

They slowed down, waited for Derry to catch up.

"What's Dooley up to?" asked David.

"Dribbling, probably," said Drew. "Cor—just look at the fistful he's got!"

Dooley had gone off a little way beyond the school gates, clutching his ice creams. He leaned against a tree, looked down at them longingly, the ice cream already melting and running down his hands. Then, to their astonishment, he threw the lot into the undergrowth, and walked away.

The three stood in shocked silence.

"Are you thinking what I'm thinking?" Derry asked of David.

David nodded.

"What a waste!" said Drew.

"We've got to get him near a mirror," said Derry. "If he doesn't show up in there . . ."

"It'll be because someone's turned the mirror round," laughed Drew.

"But he didn't eat the ice cream," said Derry.

"So?" said Drew. "Maybe he was feeling sick—running in the hot sun."

"Sun?" said David quickly. "You saw him run in the sun?"

"Sure," said Drew. "*And* he cast a shadow."

"Did you see it?" asked David.

"Well, no, but—well, he must have done! Heck, Dave, I've had enough of Dooley himself this morning without having his shadow to watch out for as well! Now come on! I can eat some ice cream even if he can't!"

"Whose group was Dooley in?" demanded Big Sir.

"Mine, sir," David said.

"When did you last see him?"

"Just before lunch, sir. He was buying ice cream. Then he walked away, presumably home to lunch."

"Who else was in your group?"

"Derry and Andrew."

"Andrew—when did you see him last?"

"Same time as David, sir."

"Me, too," said Derry.

"Whose group was Wigmore in?" asked Big Sir.

"Mine, sir," said David.

"Do you happen to know where *he* is?"

"No, sir."

"All right. We must carry on without them. David, Derry, Andrew—please stay behind afterwards."

When the bell rang, the class handed in their papers and scrambled out. The three Ds remained in their seats.

"Have any of you other classes this period?" asked Big Sir.

"I'm due for carpentry," said Drew.

"Well, you'd better not miss that. Derry?"

"Domestic science, sir. I don't mind missing that."

"I'm sure you don't," said Big Sir. "But off you go!"

Reluctantly, Derry and Drew left.

"David—you have a free period?"

"Yes, sir."

"Good. Now—about Dooley and Wigmore. Did anything untoward happen during the discussion that might have made them go missing?"

"Er—no, sir, not really."

"What was your subject?"

"Ghosts, sir."

"Hmm. Unusual. Did Dooley and Wigmore join in?"

"Oh, yes, sir," said David feelingly. And how! he thought.

"Good," said Big Sir. "What made you choose Wigmore, by the way?"

"I didn't, sir. He chose us."

"I thought it was something like that," smiled Big Sir. "I'd like to hear the tape, David."

David hesitated. "Er—well—it may sound a bit odd, sir."

"Odd?"

"It was the things Dooley said, sir." David gulped hard, wondering how it would sound to Big Sir. "He said he was a—a ghost, sir."

For a very uncomfortable moment Big Sir stared at him.

"I said," went on David hastily, "that we couldn't include remarks like that, and he said why not—that was the subject. Then Drew—no, Derry—said that he should be glad he wasn't a ghost because then he couldn't eat gallons of ice cream like he did. Then Dooley said he only pretended to eat ice cream. Then he repeated he was a ghost."

"Anything else?" asked Big Sir.

"Oh, yes, sir, lots."

"Hmm," said Big Sir. "Well, as you know, I never interfere with your choice of subject for these debates, but this appears to have gone off the rails. Perhaps I'd better hear the tape now. Start where Dooley said he was a ghost."

David took a cassette from his pocket, placed it on the desk. He switched on, carefully selecting a point on the tape. But it was David's voice that came first: "Look, Dooley, we can't include remarks like that you know."

"Sorry, sir," said David, "I didn't go back far enough." He adjusted the tape, switched on again. Silence for a while— then David's voice: "Look, Dooley, we can't include remarks like that you know."

This time, Big Sir stopped the tape. "Remarks like what, David?" he asked.

87

"What he said, sir," answered David, puzzled.

"I haven't heard him say *anything* yet!"

"I don't understand it, sir. Shall I go back?"

"No." Big Sir switched on again. "Let it run."

There was a silence for a moment, then came Derry's voice: "Bet you're glad you're *not*. Ghosts can't gollop ice cream by the gallon!" Another silence, then Drew's voice, jeering: "Oh yes?" A longer pause followed. They waited, unspeaking, David uncomfortably aware of Big Sir's gaze upon him.

Then came Derry's voice, saying: "Seriously, though, Dooley. Do *you* believe in ghosts?" Silence; then Drew's voice: "Oh sure. If I pushed you, my hand would go right through you." Shortly followed by, "You're no ghost, old son! You can't get out of maths that way."

Another brief pause followed, then Drew's voice again: "So why do you bother?" Another silence, then David's voice saying: "Anyone else got any points to raise?" "Can't think of anything," from Derry. "Drew?" asked David. And finally they heard Drew say: "Except that there's no such things as ghosts. Or if there are—we don't believe in 'em!"

David switched off the tape. "I switched off after that, sir," he said shakily, "but Dooley went on talking."

"*Went on* talking!" said Big Sir. "You know, David, I don't like practical jokes."

"He *did* say those things, sir," protested David. "And more, after I'd switched off. But we were getting ready for lunch and we didn't take much notice."

"But I thought you bought ice creams first?"

"Oh yes, sir. So did Dooley. But he threw his away."

"Well, maybe his uncle had warned him off. I shall have to stop the ice cream van calling just before lunch." Big Sir paused, thinking, then he said: "This tape hasn't been out of your possession since the discussion?"

"No, sir."

"So Dooley couldn't have got hold of it, blanked out his voice?"

"No chance, sir."

"Are you *sure* the recorder was on while Dooley was speaking?"

"Certain, sir. All the time."

"It could have been switched off accidentally."

"Hardly likely, sir. Not all those times."

"Are you sure you didn't switch off *deliberately* during Dooley's silly talk?"

"I am sure, sir," answered David firmly. "You think it *was* silly talk?"

"I haven't heard him say anything yet, David!"

David switched on, ran the tape back, then forward again, turning up the sound. In the silences between their three recorded voices could be heard the murmur of other groups, a bird sang somewhere, an ice cream van chimed in the distance.

David's face was pale, his eyes puzzled. Not, thought Big Sir, the face of one who had played a practical joke or was desperately trying to cover one up.

"And there was something else, sir," David was saying. "Wiggy—er Wigmore—claims he was pushed. But there was no one near him."

"What has this to do with Dooley's ghost talk?"

"Well, just before, Dooley had said he could prove he was a ghost by not being there. Then Wiggy started acting up and we forgot all about Dooley. When we looked round for him—he'd gone."

"You think he pushed Wigmore then ran like the wind?"

"No one pushed Wiggy," said David firmly.

Big Sir was silent.

"Sir," ventured David, "if Dooley *is* a ghost, his voice *wouldn't* be recorded, would it?"

"Neither would he show up in mirrors or cast a shadow in the sun, eh?" asked Big Sir.

"He did pass the non-eating test."

"There could be a simple explanation to that. He probably

felt sick and stayed home. He's played truant several times before, you know. Meanwhile, say nothing about this." Big Sir indicated the tape.

"No, sir. But sir—to be a ghost, you have to be dead, don't you?"

"Yes," said Big Sir quietly. "I'm afraid you do."

"Not on it!" said Derry and Drew simultaneously.

"Just blank spaces," said David. "Nothing where his voice should be."

"You're having us on!" said Drew. "All that ghost talk's got to you."

"I'm not joking," said David.

"Well then," said Drew, "you erased Dooley's voice."

"When? I went to lunch with you, came straight back into class with you."

"Could Dooley have got hold of it?" asked Derry.

"How?" asked David. "It's been with me all the time. No one erased it, anyway. You can hear the background sounds."

"He could have recorded those while we were at lunch," put in Drew.

"But he couldn't have got hold of the tape!" insisted David.

"So, it must have had a defect," retorted Drew. "It failed to record in those places."

"It was a new tape," said David.

"That's right," said Derry, her voice excited. "No one edited it, and there are blank spaces where Dooley's voice should be!"

"That doesn't make him a ghost," said Drew stubbornly.

"It does, it does!" said Derry.

"Rubbish!" scoffed Drew. "Just because he threw away his ice creams? I bet his uncle warned him not to eat before lunch or he'd get a hiding—but *couldn't* eat them?—no! And again, no, no and no!"

90

"Yes, yes and yes!" said Derry.

"Bosh!" said Drew rudely. "Poppycock and balderdash! as Wiggy's dad would say. For once I agree with that idiot's dad. Ghosts just *aren't*. Dooley's missing because he funked a maths mock when he saw how hard it was."

"What do you mean—when he saw how hard it was?" demanded David quickly.

"Well, he was there for a while."

"But you told Big Sir you hadn't seen him since the group session."

"I hadn't then," said Drew. "It was only after the exam started. He was sitting at his desk behind you."

"Then others must have seen him."

"Unlikely," said Drew. "They all had their heads down— even Derry. Me—I was wandering as usual, loath to get to grips with the beastly paper."

"Did you see him come in through the door?" asked Derry.

"Closed or open?" grinned Drew. "Sorry to disappoint you, sis, but I just looked up and saw him at his desk. I don't think even Big Sir saw him—his head was well down, too. When I looked up again, Dooley wasn't there any more."

"But he *couldn't* have come and gone," said David, "without disturbing any of us."

"Why not?" asked Drew. "He sneaked in quietly so Big Sir wouldn't notice, sat down, found the exam too much for him—as usual—then disappeared again."

"But someone must have seen him go out," insisted David.

"When has anyone," said Drew, "had time to look up once stuck into one of Big Sir's exam papers? Takes all my concentration trying to discover what it's all about even! But I *did* see Dooley before I dived in."

"It's odd," said David. "Only *you* saw him."

"Maybe I'm psychic!" grinned Drew.

"Are you sure you saw him, Drew?" David asked.

"Yep. Didn't keep my eyes on him, of course—there was

the beastly paper to struggle with. Besides, there was one heck of a draught whistling down my neck. I felt thoroughly miserable, I can tell you."

"That's strange," said David. "I felt that, too. Kind of cold air. How about you, Derry?"

She nodded. "Come to think of it, I did."

"It was a very warm day," said David. "The windows were open but there was no breeze."

"I was going to ask," said Derry, "if I could move, when it suddenly stopped. Did yours stop, Drew?"

"Don't know," said Drew. "I put my coat collar up."

"Mine didn't stop," said David. "I felt it for practically the whole of the exam."

"He was there!" said Derry suddenly, in an awed voice. "Dooley was there all the time!"

"Cheating, no doubt?" grinned Drew.

"Maybe," said Derry.

Drew exploded into laughter. "Oh, my twitty twin!" he gasped. "A ghost copying our papers?"

"Not yours!" said Derry with sisterly contempt. "He hung around you till he realized you'd be no good to him. Then he came over to me—where, I confess, he didn't do much better—and then to David, where he stayed."

"Well, I've heard everything," laughed Drew. He was still laughing when Big Sir came in.

"I am glad," said Big Sir dryly, "that you are in good spirits, Andrew."

"Spirits!" gasped Drew. "Excuse me, sir, but that's very appropriate in the circumstances!"

"I presume," said Big Sir, "you are thinking of Dooley?"

"He was there, sir!" said Derry quickly. "In the classroom. Drew saw him."

"Yes, but he didn't stay, sir," said Drew.

"Hmm," said Big Sir. "He must have slipped in and out while I was busy."

"Then you think he was just playing truant after all?"

Derry sounded disappointed.

"It looks like it," said Big Sir, cautiously. "Wigmore, by the way, went home—not feeling well. But his father sent him back. Now what are you all doing in your classroom? Haven't you a lesson to go to?"

"We just came to collect some things," said David.

"Well, hurry up!"

"Sir," asked David, "will you tell Dooley's uncle this time?"

"Let us hope," said Big Sir, "that he will turn up of his own accord."

"Do *you* believe he's a ghost, sir?" asked Drew bluntly.

"If I say I do," replied Big Sir, "would you think I was approaching, if not actually round, the proverbial bend?"

"Well, sir—"

"There are many things in life, Andrew, that we do not understand. To scoff at them is ignorance, to say the least."

"Yes, sir," said Drew, "but—well—Dooley, a ghost! It's ridiculous! He's just trying to draw attention to himself."

Was that it? thought Big Sir. Or was it something deeper . . . urgent . . . frightening?

"Well," said Big Sir, "maybe he'll come back before school is over."

"Of course he will," said Drew. "Lot of fuss about nothing, if you ask me!"

Depressed by the evident ignorance of so many of his pupils, Big Sir looked up from the exam papers, looked out on the bright day. What, he thought, would he say to Dooley's uncle should he be forced to see him? "Mr Larson, we have reason to believe that your nephew is a ghost!"

The playing fields looked quiet and peaceful in the warm summer noon. Beneath the trees flanking the fields a small, lone figure walked. He looked weary, dejected, sad. Even from this distance Big Sir could see that it was Dooley.

The boy was on the edge of the fields now. Was he coming in?

93

Big Sir got up, opened the window wide and called, "Dooley!"

The boy looked up sharply.

"Dooley!" Big Sir called again. "Will you come to me, please?"

The boy hesitated a second, then started to walk towards the school entrance. Big Sir came back into the room and waited. Presently the door opened and Dooley walked in.

"Where have you been?" asked Big Sir.

"I—I'm not sure, sir," said Dooley.

There was no impudence in his manner. Could it be amnesia—or some other form of illness? thought Big Sir. He put out a hand to touch his shoulder. For one brief moment that was no time at all, Big Sir felt nothing. Then his fingers became sensitive to cloth, the hard shoulder. A boy? he thought. Or a ghost? A ghost who could appear solid when touched but had been slow to identify, to become solid—as it were—for the one who touched him?

"You missed the mock maths exam," said Big Sir. "There is no shame in failing, Dooley; only in not trying. Your granny would have wanted you to try."

"Yes, I know," said Dooley.

"You're not sick, are you?"

Dooley shook his head. "Are you—are you going to tell my uncle, sir?"

"I don't know," said Big Sir. He glanced momentarily out of the window. A group of pupils were heading for the main gates. He had not heard the chimes but he guessed the ice cream van was in the vicinity. *Ice cream*! The children had said . . .

"By the way, Dooley—" he began, then stopped.

The room was empty.

First he was startled, then angry. The boy had not been dismissed. There were certain rules of politeness, respect. He strode towards the door, opened it quickly. A startled Wigmore fell into the room.

"Wigmore! What are you doing? Were you listening, boy?"

"N—no, sir!" Wigmore was indignant. "I was just coming in, sir. I didn't know you were here."

"What have you come for?"

"M—my apple, sir. In my desk."

"Get it then! No, wait! Did you see Dooley come out of here?"

"Dooley, sir? No, sir. Nobody came out."

"But you must have seen him, boy! He's only just this second left."

Wigmore was staring at him as if he'd gone mad.

"All right, Wigmore, get your apple and go."

Wiggy hurried to his desk, opened it, rummaged inside. Suddenly the lid came down with a bang. He howled with pain. Big Sir rushed to him and lifted the desk lid. "You should have made sure it was fastened back properly!" he said impatiently.

"I did!" sobbed Wiggy.

"Come along to the First Aid room. I'll put something on your hands."

Wiggy, his hands hanging limply at his sides in an exaggerated gesture of pain, allowed himself to be shepherded from the room. Just outside the door, he shot suddenly forward as though he'd tripped.

"What *are* you doing, Wigmore?" asked Big Sir angrily.

"You pushed me!" said Wiggy, outraged.

"*I* pushed you?" said Big Sir, astonished. "You staggered. I think you really must be ill, boy. Now come along!" He went to take Wiggy's arm.

"No sir, no sir!" Wiggy backed away from him. "I can go on my own, sir." He scuttled down the corridor.

Very disturbed now, Big Sir re-entered the classroom. Wigmore *should* have seen Dooley. Why hadn't he then? And Wigmore had thought that *he* had pushed him! And that business of the desk lid—it had fallen hard, viciously almost, as if someone had deliberately . . . He blocked his mind to

95

the possible solutions and took out the exam papers.

He worked for a while, heartened by the fact that he had come to the better entries. At least his pupils were not a total loss! That was David's—a good paper; some mistakes, but not many. Ah, the last one! He looked at the top for the name.

The name was Dooley.

Before going into the classroom, Derry paused before the large mirror in the corridor. Wiggy was right, she thought ruefully. Her hair did look a mess!

"You hair is pretty," said a voice behind her. She turned quickly. Dooley! She tried to speak, but her voice was lost way back in the dry, dry throat. *She hadn't seen him come up behind her*! She looked quickly in the mirror again. No! She could not see him! Again she turned to face him. But he was gone.

It couldn't be! she thought. He must have been standing at such an angle that he didn't show up in the mirror. But no! He'd been standing right in front of the clock. You could see *that* in the mirror.

"Hi, Derry!" called Drew from the end of the corridor. "Dooley's back. What price your old ghostie now, old girl?"

She saw Dooley now, coming from the other direction.

"Hi, Dooley!" called Drew, running up to him. "Scared any good people lately?"

"No," said Dooley. "Just Wiggy."

"Fine!" said Drew. "That's the sort of clot you want to go after. What did you do? Clank a few chains, groan in his thick ear?" He guffawed merrily. "My word, you nipped in and out of maths pretty quick didn't you, old son? Are you dead, Dooley?"

"I'm not sure," answered Dooley slowly. "The last thing I remember was being somewhere near water."

"Does your uncle know about you?" grinned Drew.

"No," said Dooley quickly, almost eagerly. "Are you going to tell him?"

96

"Not a ghost of a chance!" said Drew. "I don't think he'd appreciate a joke like that." He caught sight of Derry and David. "Hi, kids, be with you in a sec." He turned back to Dooley. "If I were you . . ." But he was talking to an empty corridor.

"What's the matter?" asked Drew as he joined Derry and David. "You look as if you've seen a ghost."

"We have," said Derry. "So have you. You've just been talking to one!"

"Oh, sure!" said Drew derisively. "Do you know, I asked him if he was dead—"

"You didn't!" gasped Derry.

"I did. And he said he wasn't sure. He's a kook all right!"

"He doesn't show up in the mirror, Drew," said David.

"What? Oh, Dave!"

"He *doesn't*!" said Derry. "Look, stand in front of the clock, Drew."

"What for?"

"Stand there and shut up!" said David gruffly.

Surprised into silence, Drew stood in front of the clock.

"Can you see yourself in the mirror?" asked Derry.

"Course I can!"

She stood in front of him, a little to one side.

"Still see yourself?"

"Not all of me," said Drew. "Not with your great bulk stuck in the way!"

"But you can see you're there?"

"Sure. I'm no ghostie, ducky."

"Well," said Derry, "Dooley was standing right where you are and I didn't see *him* in the mirror."

"Then he couldn't have been standing exactly in this spot," said Drew. He stepped to one side. "If he was here, say, you *couldn't* have seen his reflection."

"He was in front of the clock," insisted Derry crossly.

"No chance!" said Drew.

"Then get this," said David. "And I've had this from Big

97

Sir himself. Dooley turned in a maths paper after all!"

"Eh? Well, I told you he was there. He must have gone off somewhere, completed his paper, slipped it in with the others later. You see, I've solved the mystery!"

"Nothing's solved," said David. "His paper was an identical copy of mine; the same correct answers, same mistakes as well. And he couldn't have got hold of my paper after the lessons because they were all locked in Big Sir's desk."

"Well, he got to it somehow, didn't he?" said Drew. "Anyway, no problem for a ghost—oh no, of course not, that's exactly what we're arguing about, isn't it! Well, he could have unlocked the desk, pinched your paper and returned it later with his own."

"If," put in Derry, "he was clever enough to steal Sir's keys. The desk hadn't been forced. Besides, Big Sir was in the classroom all the time, and even a ghost couldn't snatch the papers from under his nose."

"But he could have copied mine," said David, "*during* the exam, then slipped his own in with the others—perhaps later, when Big Sir called him into the classroom."

"Okay," said Drew. "But *why*? Why should he want to pass a maths exam?"

"To please his granny," said Derry.

"It's ridiculous!" scoffed Drew.

"It's frightening," said Derry.

"We can settle this!" David said. "Go see his uncle."

"Oh no!" Derry was horrified. "We daren't!"

"What's there to be scared of?" asked Drew. "I'm game."

"We'll go this evening," said David.

"Right!" said Drew. "Though I don't know what you expect to find."

David was silent. It was more a question of what he was *afraid* to find.

They stopped at the farm road to the house. It loomed large, the dirt of years about it, an ugly, sprawling building with

98

small, grubby windows peering out from thick walls of grimy grey slate.

"I couldn't live *here*!" shuddered Derry.

"A house for ghosts to walk in!" whispered Drew. "And little boys to die in!"

"Stop it!" said Derry. "You are morbid!"

Drew chuckled. "We're on a ghost hunt, aren't we? Foul play, murder, and all that sort of merry thing?"

"Let's go home!" said Derry.

"No," said Drew. "We came here to see Dooley. If he's home, then he's no ghost and he's been having us all on, including Big Sir. *And* he's been cheating. I'm going up to the house."

"We'll all go," said David. "And let me do the talking!"

"Aye, aye, Captain!" said Drew.

They opened the gate, walked slowly up the rough road. David knocked at the great old door. It was the sort of door, thought Derry, that would creak when opened and no one would be seen to open it, and a mysterious butler looking like Vincent Price would appear as if from nowhere and say . . .

"Who are you? What do you want?"

Derry would have run, if she could have got her legs to understand what she wanted them to do. Even Drew stepped back at the sight of the huge man towering over them. But David stood his ground before Goliath.

The man's eyes gleamed in the dusk. His voice was harsh, rough. Every bit, thought Derry, of what a wicked uncle should look like.

"Good evening, sir," said David. "We're from Whitegates School. We're friends of your nephew, Mr Larson."

The hard, piercing eyes searched their faces.

"I have no nephew at Whitegates," he growled.

"But he says you're his uncle and that he lives here," said David.

They all noted the sudden jerk of his head, the involuntary

99

step backwards—the retreat of shock, as Derry afterwards put it.

"*Lives* here?" said Larson sharply.

Derry's sharp ears caught the stressed word. The *wrong* word! If, as he claimed, Dooley didn't live here, the accent should have been on the word *here* !

He glared down at them all suspiciously. "Look here, you kids, is this some sort of a practical joke?"

"Not at all, sir," said David calmly. "His name's Sam Dooley and he says you're his uncle."

He's afraid! thought Derry. And so was she! They shouldn't have come here alone, enquiring after Dooley. Playing their hand, she believed it was called. Now the uncle knew they *knew*!

"But, sir—" persisted David.

"Get away!" he roared. "All of you!" He slammed the door shut.

Derry started to run.

"Don't show him you're afraid, sis," said Drew.

"I am!" said Derry. "Aren't you?"

"Well," said Drew, "it's not exactly my idea of a fun evening."

"We shouldn't have come," said Derry.

"Rubbish!" Drew was more confident now he was outside the gate.

"He was scared of something," said David.

"That's what I'm scared of!" said Derry.

"He was lying, anyway," said Drew. "Mind you, I can't say I blame him for disowning Dooley!"

"Don't joke!" admonished Derry. "I feel that something awful has happened in this place . . . in that house, maybe!"

"Let's go!" said David quickly. "Have a look round while it's still light enough to see."

"What are we looking for?" asked Drew.

"I don't know. Something . . . anything."

"Brilliant!" murmured Drew.

100

They were well away from the house now, but still within sight of it. David stopped suddenly. "Listen!" he said. "Can you hear anything?"

"Oh no!" said Drew. "Not that old can-you-hear-anything-no-isn't-it-quiet joke!"

"Shut up," said David, "and listen!"

They listened. A faint rushing sound came to them from beyond the tall grasses of the dusk-filled meadow.

"A weir?" asked David.

"Bull's-eye," said Drew. "Probably the water Dooley mentioned."

"What water?"

"When I was kidding him about being a ghost and dead and all that. He said the last place he remembers was being near water."

"Let's go find the river!" said David. "We won't use the torch until we're out of sight of the house."

"He couldn't see us through all this rubbish!" said Drew. "He's a rotten farmer as well as a liar!"

"Do you think," asked Derry quietly, "the river's where it happened, David?"

"Maybe."

"Where what happened?" asked Drew.

"Do I have to spell it out for you?" asked David crossly.

"You know me!" said Drew. "Ever the realist. And, man, I'm telling you we're on a wild goose chase."

David shone his torch upon the dark, swirling waters as they tumbled down over the great stones and boulders that broke the level of the river before it flowed into the woods beyond.

"This is a fast current," said David. "Dooley's body could have been washed down river, well out of sight in the woods."

Derry and Drew said nothing.

"Well," said David, "that's what we all now believe, isn't it?"

"Not me!" said Drew. "I pass. And by the looks of that sister of mine she's about to pass *out*!"

"No, I'm all right," said Derry quickly. "And I agree with David. Dooley's uncle drowned him in this river."

"Oh, yes?" scoffed Drew. "So why hasn't his body been found?"

"Because," said David, "he's hardly likely to have reported it to the police!"

"But Big Sir would have made enquiries when Dooley didn't turn up this term."

"But he *did* turn up," said Derry.

"Sure," said Drew. "But his uncle wouldn't have known he'd come back as a ghost. He would have had to consider the possibility of the school making enquiries."

"Probably had some good excuse ready," said David. "Like he'd run away."

"In which case," persisted Drew, "the police would have got around to searching the entire farm."

"He took a chance," said David. "All murderers take some chances."

"All right," said Drew. "Let's get this straight. Despite my superior judgment in these matters, you kids believe Dooley to be a ghost and that his wicked uncle killed him. So—*when* is Dooley supposed to have died?"

"Before he was a ghost, silly!" said Derry.

"Then he must have done him in during last term holidays. In which case," went on Drew thoughtfully, "he's been dead for, say . . . gosh . . . ten or eleven weeks! Drowned bodies are supposed to look horribly bloated and all that!"

"Oh!" shuddered Derry. "I hadn't thought of that! I hope we *don't* find him!"

"Unless, of course," went on Drew, "his uncle managed to retrieve it. Now there are various ways one can dispose of an unwanted body—"

"We're not looking for a body," interrupted David. "Just for anything that may have belonged to Dooley." He

102

scrambled down the bank, the others following, Drew still protesting.

The weir revealing nothing; they began to follow the river.

"Look!" said David suddenly, keeping his torch steady on a clump of bushes. "There's something sticking out."

"Well," said Drew, "it's probably only a—" he bent down, picked up something— "a fishing basket."

"Could be Dooley's," said David.

"Well, if it is," said Drew, "I hope it's not full of stinking fish!" He opened it gingerly. It was empty. "Whew! That's a relief! Can't be his, anyway. His uncle would have made a thorough search."

"It might not have occurred to him," said David, "that Dooley had a basket also—some fishermen carry only a shoulder pouch. There must be a lot of good catches in this river. Let's go on."

They walked for a while in silence. The thinning trees of the timber-plundered woodland were fast becoming tall, scraggy shadows. The river still gleamed dully beside them as David kept his torch shining along the bank.

Then Derry stopped. "Listen!" she said.

"And the next line," sighed Drew, "is—can you hear anything?"

"Well, *can* you?" asked Derry.

They paused, listened.

"S—someone's following us," whispered Derry. "I heard twigs cracking, leaves rustling . . ."

"Imagination," scoffed Drew. "I don't hear a thing. You, Dave?"

David shook his head.

"Of course you don't!" said Derry. "He stopped when we stopped. But I *heard* him."

"Uncle?" asked Drew.

"Who else?" said Derry. "Oh, let's go back!"

"And run right into him?" said Drew. "That *would* be good thinking!"

"It's probably only rabbits, Derry," said David reassuringly.

They walked on. Again Derry heard the sounds; behind them in the woods, a little to the left, as of feet treading bracken.

Darned heavy rabbits! thought Derry. But she said nothing, drew closer to the others.

They could scarcely see each other now, although the river's gleam afforded some light. The boys were intent on searching the river's edge. Without stopping, Derry looked back, listening. The wood was a darkness behind and around them, the trees crowding in as if they themselves were following. But she heard nothing. She turned, looked on ahead beyond the two boys.

"Look!" she whispered, clutching at their sleeves. "*There* —ahead of us!"

They looked, stopped.

"Well, I'll be—!" said Drew. "It's the ghost himself!"

"He's carrying a rod," said Derry.

"And—yes—see, he's wearing a pouch!" David said.

"Fishing! At this time of night!" exclaimed Drew. "Hi, Dooley!" he called. "Kind of late to be fishing, isn't it? They've all gone beddy-byes! I told you he was a kook!" he muttered. "Now perhaps we can all go home and give this ghost-hunting lark a rest?"

Dooley had raised one hand in a beckoning gesture.

"He wants us to follow him," whispered Derry.

"Not likely!" said Drew. "If he wants to do mad things like fishing at night—"

"We must!" said Derry. "If we don't help him now we shall never know the truth about him."

"And that suits me," said Drew. "Let him haunt this scraggy old forest on his own!"

While Drew had been speaking, Dooley had turned, moved away from the bank and farther on into the woods. They had to strain their eyes now to see him, but he was still there, and

104

moving. Then, as they watched, he stopped, turned, beckoned again. Then, in an instant, he was gone. He had not moved—but he was gone.

"Well, that settles it," said Drew, trying hard to be casual, but his voice was shaky. "We can't follow nothing. Let's go home."

"We should have followed him the first time," said Derry. "Now he thinks we don't want to."

"He's right," said Drew. "I don't!" He jumped suddenly. "Look, there he is again—I think!"

A mist was moving beyond the point where Dooley had last been standing. It swirled for a while then slowly moulded, resolving at last into the shape of Dooley. This time he was walking away from them, but slowly, as if fearing to walk out of their sight.

"What shall we do?" whispered Derry.

"Watch him," said David. "If he turns and beckons us on again, then we go. Fair enough, Drew?"

"Fair enough," said Drew.

Dooley had raised his arm again.

"Well, come on!" said Drew. "A ghost can't hurt us."

They followed, watching Dooley anxiously lest he should fade away from them again. They moved in a world of shadows, away from the river now and farther into the woods.

"I think I know where this leads," said David. "Used to be an old gravel pit here somewhere."

They could see Dooley plainly now, a strange and moving lightness in the darkness of the wood. They followed him until he emerged into a clearing.

David motioned them to stop. "Look where he's going!" he whispered. "He's heading straight for the gravel pit! And—by golly—it's a *flooded* gravel pit!"

"See!" gasped Derry. "Oh, look David—Drew—he's *walking* on it! *He's walking on the water!*"

"I see," said Drew, "but I don't believe it!"

105

Dooley was walking, unhurriedly, effortlessly, over the surface of the flooded gravel pit. He reached the centre, stopped, turned, faced them. He stood now motionless upon the water.

"He doesn't expect us to follow him in *there*?" gasped Drew.

In the same instant, Dooley vanished.

And then, in the stillness, they all heard it—behind them, in the woods; the cracking of twigs, of branches being brushed aside, of heavy feet trampling bracken. David grabbed Derry's arm and, pushing a startled Drew before him, he ran across the clearing to where the woods began again.

They waited fearfully, crouched low behind a clump of trees, watching the blackness which marked the edge of the wood on the other side of the clearing.

"Who is it?" whispered Derry.

"Uncle!" breathed David. "And he's got a gun!"

"Oh, no!" gasped Derry.

"He can't kill us *all*," said David stoutly.

"One is enough!" said Drew grimly.

"And I don't want to be that one!" said Derry.

"Our only chance," Drew murmured, "is to split up. Right, Dave?"

"Right! If we separate, he won't know who to aim at first. By that time we can all be lost in the wood. After that—well—he's got to be able to *see* to shoot. One of us will get away—and he daren't do anything to the other two."

"He'll try, though!" said Derry shakily.

"Much as I hate to be a hero," said Drew, "if I could run out into the clearing, it would give you two a chance to get away—fetch help . . ."

"No chance!" said David. "You'd be a running duck! And anyway, here he comes!"

Larson had emerged from the woods. He stood for a moment or two, looking towards the gravel pit.

"What sort of a ghost *is* Dooley?" whispered Drew. "Any

self-respecting spirit who knew his stuff would materialize right now—scare the wits out of old man Larson while we get away!"

"Perhaps," said Derry, "he wasn't following us at all. Just returning to the scene of his crime—the gravel pit. That's where—" she gulped—"Dooley's body is!"

"There's going to be another crime," growled Drew, "if we don't get out of here, and fast!"

Larson had turned, facing in their direction, as if he could see them where they hid, trembling, behind the clump of trees.

"He knows we're here!" whispered Derry. "He *was* following us!"

Slowly, determinedly, Larson began to come towards them.

"If we could make it back to the river . . ." began Drew.

"No time!" snapped David. "Scatter and run!"

They ran in three different directions, plunging into the woods behind them, running wildly, blindly . . .

"He can get us all!" sobbed Derry, already feeling the thump of a bullet in her back. She could hear the great feet crashing and thundering behind her, the swish of the ruthlessly parted bracken, the cracking of twigs and branches. He was following *her*!

She ran on through the darkness, stifling her scream, lest he should know for sure just where to aim the gun. She bumped into something—something hard, something high and very wide and solid. Two great arms enfolded her, lifting her off her feet, then set her aside swiftly but gently.

Big Sir met the swift onslaught of Larson full on. His huge arms wrapped round the hurtling figure, his knee came up in a sharp jab to the man's stomach. Larson groaned and slumped to the ground, the gun falling away from him.

"David—Drew!" called Derry. "It's all right, Big Sir's got him!"

They came running. Drew picked up the gun.

"Give that to me," said Big Sir. "It might go off!" Drew hastily handed it over. "Get up!" said Big Sir, prodding Larson.

Still groaning, Larson scrambled up.

"Dooley brought us to the gravel pit," said Derry. "That's where we think he's—buried."

"Is that right, Larson?" asked Big Sir.

Larson's eyes were wide and glittering in the darkness. "D—Dooley brought you?" he stuttered, staring at Derry. "B—but he's—"

"Dead, Larson?" asked Big Sir.

"I'm saying nothing!" growled Larson.

"Well," said Big Sir, "the police will search the gravel pit in the morning. We'll know then."

"Can we come?" asked Drew excitedly.

"Certainly not! This is no work for children!"

"Oh, no, it's *not* sir!" said Derry fervently.

As they passed the gravel pit, Derry shuddered, tried not to think of what might lie beneath. She wondered if Dooley's ghost would appear again. But the waters lay smooth, silent, unruffled in the darkness. And no light shone and nothing moved upon the cold, still surface.

Swiftly, she followed Big Sir and the boys.

"Well," said Big Sir, "they did find poor Dooley's body in the gravel pit. As you may have guessed, he'd been there some time."

"Oh, dear!" said Derry, trying hard not to picture it.

"He says he didn't deliberately kill the boy. They were arguing about boarding school when Dooley slipped and fell in."

"Boarding school?" they chorused.

"When Dooley's granny died last term and he went to live with his uncle, Larson informed me he'd be sending Dooley to a boarding school. I tried to dissuade him—thought I had when Dooley turned up as usual this term—as a ghost!"

"How did you explain how we got on to it, sir?" asked David.

"That was tricky. I didn't lie—just didn't tell the whole truth. Otherwise, they might well have locked me up with Larson! I said you had visited Dooley's uncle, enquiring how he was getting on at boarding school, that Larson had acted suspiciously, which sent you off on the trail. Anyway, Larson's full confession means that there will be no extensive enquiries. The police may, of course, want your side of it."

"Which will, of course, be the same as yours, sir," said David stoutly.

"But what about the rest of the school?" asked Drew. "They've all seen Dooley."

"I doubt," said Big Sir, "if Dooley appeared anywhere outside your classroom. Your classmates knew he was missing, of course. If they hear about his death they'll be sorry—I hope—but I doubt if they will question the circumstances—unless they are all like you!"

"He was outside in the grounds with our group, sir," said David. "And visible."

"But only to you," said Big Sir.

"Wiggy saw him," said David.

"And *felt* him," grinned Drew.

"That's because Wiggy insulted me," said Derry proudly.

"Wigmore," said Big Sir dryly, "is not likely to concern himself with Dooley's disappearance. And even if he did put two and two together it's extremely unlikely he'd come up with the right answer!"

"Well, *I* don't believe it *was* an accident," said Derry. "Larson hated Dooley, he was an extra burden. Motive enough for murder, surely?"

"Maybe," said Big Sir, "but it is not for us to judge."

"But sir," said David, "surely Larson realized someone would have missed Dooley?"

"No. Apart from his uncle, his granny was his only relative."

"He shouldn't have tried to cover it up," said Derry.

"No, but he panicked. He thought no one would believe it was an accident. He managed to pull the boy out of the river, but he was already dead. So, in his fear, he buried the body in the old gravel pit in his woods. And that, so he thought, was that."

"Except he hadn't bargained for Dooley's ghoulie!" said Drew.

"Or the extra fishing basket," said David.

"It was his granny," said Derry, "who really started things rolling. That's why she sent Dooley back to our school—after he was dead. She suspected his uncle of polishing him off, but couldn't do much about it herself. Ghosts need living people to find out things for them. That's why Dooley kept disappearing—to get us to stir things up."

"Which we sure did," said Drew.

"David and *I* did!" said Derry. "*You* wouldn't believe he was a ghost till you'd seen him disappear before your very eyes!"

"Nevertheless," said Big Sir, "you shouldn't have gone to the farm on your own. You gave Larson a great shock, enquiring after his nephew. He thought the police had found something, set a trap. Partly my fault, of course. When I mistakenly told David that Dooley had turned in a maths paper identical to his own I should have guessed you'd all become ghost hunters with a vengeance!"

"How did you find us?" asked David.

"I called on Larson," said Big Sir. "He was out."

"After us!" said Derry.

"With a gun!" added David.

"And murder in his heart!" said Drew with relish.

"Happily," said Big Sir, "I saw him heading for the river. I came into the woods by the opposite way, hoping to reach you first."

"Which you did!" said Derry fervently.

"It was a near thing!" said Drew darkly.

"Do you think, sir?" asked David, "he *would* have shot us?"

"I think he would have," declared Derry. "He could have claimed he thought we were poachers."

"Poachers!" scoffed Drew. "In that scraggy old wod? Couldn't bag a brace of bumble bees!"

"I don't know," said Big Sir. "I wasn't waiting to find out! But right now," he grinned, "it's lesson time. Education waits for no man!"

"Or ghost!" said Drew.

"Poor Dooley!" murmured Derry.

"Poor nothing!" exclaimed Drew. "No more maths for him, and he's with his granny again. Only thing I regret is there'll be no ghostie to push Wiggy around any more."

"No more draughts in the classroom either," said Derry.

"And no one," said David, "to crib my papers."

"I wouldn't bank on that," said Drew as he opened the classroom door. "Look where Wiggy's sitting now!"

"Oh, no!" groaned David. "Don't tell me I've got to put up with *him* behind me!"

"Wonder what he'd say," whispered Drew, "if he knew he was sitting in the seat of a ghost?"

"I have a strange feeling," murmured Derry, "that he *will* know!"

"Please, sir," said Wiggy, "may I move, sir?"

"Move, Wigmore? But you've just done that!"

"Yes, sir. But I'd like to move back, sir!"

"I thought you always wanted that desk by the window?"

"Yes, sir. But there's a draught, sir!"

"Don't be ridiculous, boy! On a day like this?"

"Please, sir, there is, sir. May I move, sir?"

"You shouldn't have sat there without permission," said Big Sir sternly. "Now you can stay there."

The class went on for five minutes, disturbed only by the constant mutterings of Wiggy, who sat with his coat collar

111

up. At one point, when Derry was watching him, she saw his hair blowing wildly, as if in a wind. She caught Drew's eye. They sat, fascinated, watching Wiggy's discomfiture. Suddenly he let out a yell and tumbled out of his seat on to the floor.

"Wigmore! What *are* you doing?"

"Someone pushed me, sir!" yelled Wiggy.

"Wigmore—if I have any more nonsense about pushing—" He stopped, having caught David's eye. "Oh, well, perhaps you'd better go back to your own desk. *No!* Don't move your belongings! Just go!"

But Wiggy already had the desk lid up, was hastily collecting his possessions. The lid fell down with a bang that was no louder than Wiggy's yell of rage and pain.

"I suppose you think that's funny!" he roared at David between his moans of pain.

"Who—me?" asked David. "Why, I—" He stopped, seeing Drew and Derry convulsed with silent laughter.

"It was your own carelessness, Wigmore," said Big Sir sternly. "Now go along to the First Aid room and stay there, so the rest of us can pass what's left of this lesson in peace!"

Still groaning, and glaring at the class in general, Wiggy scuttled from the room.

They settled down with his going, and only the scratching of pens on paper sounded in the warm, quiet summer afternoon.

Derry looked up once, saw Big Sir gazing at the vacant desk behind David. A slight breeze, soft as a sigh, ruffled her hair, played for a while about her face, and then was gone.

Goodbye, Dooley! she whispered without sound. She looked over at Drew. His head was well down over his papers, his brow furrowed with either concentration or despair. For a moment, he raised his eyes, his head half turned, as if someone had touched his shoulder. She caught his questioning eye, nodded. They both looked over at David, who was, as usual, writing easily, calmly. Then he, too, looked up, his

112

hand half raised, as if in a gesture of goodbye.

The three Ds smiled at each other, then went back to their lessons.

Beyond the white gates, the old ice cream man played his chimes, prepared his wares and waited.

They drifted effortlessly through the gates and, for a moment, parted. Dooley, visible in his longing, paused beside the van for one last look at the cool delights of the living. A little way off, the old lady waited with understanding love.

"Off at last, then, lad?" asked the ice cream man. He noted Dooley's longing look at his wares. "I'd give you one," he said, "but what's the use? Let's leave them for those who can."

"Why do *you* stay?" asked Dooley.

"Habits one likes are hard to break," said the old man.

"You're telling me!" said Dooley.

The old man smiled, gently, encouragingly. "Don't worry, son! Unlike me, you'll soon learn to adjust. The young ones always do."

"Will you play the chimes again?" asked Dooley.

"Sure will!" said the old man. "Least I can do to send you on your way."

The chimes rang out in clear and joyful melody, sounding sweet upon the warm air of the bright, bright day.

Warm and happy in the sun, they walked unhurriedly along the summer-scented road, a boy and his granny—two ghosts who looked like people, two people who were ghosts.

7 The Judge's House
Bram Stoker

When the time for his examination drew near Malcolm Malcolmson made up his mind to go somewhere to read by himself. He feared the attractions of the seaside, and also he feared completely rural isolation, for of old he knew its charms, and so he determined to find some unpretentious little town where there would be nothing to distract him. He refrained from asking suggestions from any of his friends, for he argued that each would recommend some place of which he had knowledge and where he had already acquaintances. As Malcolmson wished to avoid friends he had no wish to encumber himself with the attention of friends' friends, and so he determined to look out for a place for himself. He packed a portmanteau with some clothes and all the books he required, and then took ticket for the first name on the local time-table which he did not know.

When at the end of three hours' journey he alighted at Benchurch, he felt satisfied that he had so far obliterated his tracks as to be sure of having a peaceful opportunity of pursuing his studies. He went straight to the one inn which the sleepy little place contained, and put up for the night. Benchurch was a market town, and once in three weeks was crowded to excess, but for the remainder of the twenty-one days it was as attractive as a desert. Malcolmson looked around the day after his arrival to try to find quarters more isolated than even so quiet an inn as The Good Traveller afforded. There was only one place which took his fancy, and it certainly satisfied his wildest ideas regarding quiet; in fact, quiet was not the proper word to apply to it—desolation was the only term conveying any suitable idea of its isolation. It was an old rambling, heavy-built house of the Jacobean style, with heavy gables and windows, unusually small, and set higher than was customary in such houses, and was surrounded with a high brick wall massively built. Indeed, on examination, it looked more like a fortified house than an ordinary dwelling. But all these things pleased Malcolmson. Here, he thought, is the very spot I have been looking for, and if I can get the opportunity of using it I shall be happy. His joy was increased when he realized beyond doubt that it was not at present inhabited.

From the post-office he got the name of the agent, who was really surprised at the application to rent a part of the old house. Mr Carnford, the local lawyer and agent, was a genial old gentleman, and frankly confessed his delight at anyone being willing to live in the house.

"To tell you the truth," said he, "I should be only too happy, on behalf of the owners, to let anyone have the house rent free for a term of years if only to accustom the people here to see it inhabited. It has been so long empty that some kind of absurd prejudice has grown up about it, and this can be best put down by its occupation—if only," he added with a sly glance at Malcolmson, "by a scholar like yourself, who wants its quiet for a time."

Malcolmson thought it needless to ask the agent about the "absurd prejudice"; he knew he would get more information, if he should require it, on that subject from other quarters.

He paid his three months' rent, got a receipt, and the name of an old woman who would probably undertake to "do" for him, and came away with the keys in his pocket. He then went to the landlady of the inn, who was a cheerful and most kindly person, and asked her advice as to such stores and provisions as he would be likely to require. She threw up her hands in amazement when he told her where he was going to settle himself.

"Not in the Judge's House!" she said, and grew pale as she spoke. He explained the locality of the house, saying that he did not know its name. When he had finished she answered:

"Aye, sure enough—sure enough the very place! It is the Judge's House sure enough." He asked her to tell him about the place, why so called, and what there was against it. She told him that it was so called locally because it had been many years before—how long she could not say, as she was herself from another part of the country, but she thought it must have been a hundred years or more—the abode of a judge who was held in great terror on account of his harsh sentences and his hostility to prisoners at Assizes. As to what there was against the house itself she could not tell. She had often asked, but no one could inform her; but there was a general feeling that there was *something*, and for her own part she would not take all the money in Drinkwater's Bank and stay in the house an hour by herself. Then she apologized to Malcolmson for her disturbing talk.

"It is too bad of me, sir, and you—and a young gentleman, too—if you will pardon me saying it, going to live there all alone. If you were my boy—and you'll excuse me for saying it—you wouldn't sleep there a night, not if I had to go there myself and pull the big alarm bell that's on the roof!" The good creature was so manifestly in earnest, and was so kindly in her intentions, that Malcolmson, although amused, was touched. He told her kindly how much he appreciated her interest in him, and added:

"But, my dear Mrs Witham, indeed you need not be

concerned about me! A man who is reading for the Mathematical Tripos has too much to think of to be disturbed by any of these mysterious 'somethings', and his work is of too exact and prosaic a kind to allow of his having any corner in his mind for mysteries of any kind. Harmonical Progression, Permutations and Combinations, and Elliptic Functions have sufficient mysteries for me!" Mrs Witham kindly undertook to see after his commissions, and he went himself to look for the old woman who had been recommended to him. When he returned to the Judge's House with her, after an interval of a couple of hours, he found Mrs Witham herself waiting with several men and boys carrying parcels, and an upholsterer's man with a bed in a car, for she said, though tables and chairs might be all very well, a bed that hadn't been aired for mayhap fifty years was not proper for young bones to lie on. She was evidently curious to see the inside of the house; and though manifestly so afraid of the "somethings" that at the slightest sound she clutched on to Malcolmson, whom she never left for a moment, went over the whole place.

After his examination of the house, Malcolmson decided to take up his abode in the great dining-room, which was big enough to serve for all his requirements; and Mrs Witham, with the aid of the charwoman, Mrs Dempster, proceeded to arrange matters. When the hampers were brought in and unpacked, Malcolmson saw that with much kind forethought she had sent from her own kitchen sufficient provisions to last for a few days. Before going she expressed all sorts of kind wishes; and at the door turned and said:

"And perhaps, sir, as the room is big and draughty it might be well to have one of those big screens put round your bed at night—though, truth to tell, I would die myself if I were to be so shut in with all kinds of—of 'things', that put their heads round the sides, or over the top, and look on me!" The image which she had called up was too much for her nerves, and she fled incontinently.

Mrs Dempster sniffed in a superior manner as the landlady disappeared, and remarked that for her own part she wasn't afraid of all the bogies in the kingdom.

"I'll tell you what it is, sir," she said. "Bogies is all kinds and sorts of things—except bogies! Rats and mice, and beetles; and creaky doors, and loose slates, and broken panes, and stiff drawer handles, that stay out when you pull them and then fall down in the middle of the night. Look at the wainscot of the room! It is old—hundreds of years old! Do you think there's no rats and beetles there? And do you imagine, sir, that you won't see none of them? Rats is bogies, I tell you, and bogies is rats; and don't you get to think anything else!"

"Mrs Dempster," said Malcolmson gravely, making her a polite bow, "you know more than a Senior Wrangler! And let me say, that, as a mark of esteem for your indubitable soundness of head and heart, I shall, when I go, give you possession of this house, and let you stay here by yourself for the last two months of my tenancy, for four weeks will serve my purpose."

"Thank you kindly, sir!" she answered, "but I couldn't sleep away from home a night. I am in Greenhow's Charity, and if I slept a night away from my rooms I should lose all I have got to live on. The rules is very strict; and there's too many watching for a vacancy for me to run any risks in the matter. Only for that, sir, I'd gladly come here and attend on you altogether during your stay."

"My good woman," said Malcolmson hastily, "I have come here on purpose to obtain solitude; and believe me that I am grateful to the late Greenhow for having so organized his admirable charity—whatever it is—that I am perforce denied the opportunity of suffering from such a form of temptation! Saint Anthony himself could not be more rigid on the point!"

The old woman laughed harshly. "Ah, you young gentlemen," she said, "you don't fear for naught; and belike you'll

118

get all the solitude you want here." She set to work with her cleaning; and by nightfall, when Malcolmson returned from his walk—he always had one of his books to study as he walked—he found the room swept and tidied, a fire burning in the old hearth, the lamp lit, and the table spread for supper with Mrs Witham's excellent fare. "This is comfort, indeed," he said, as he rubbed his hands.

When he had finished his supper, and lifted the tray to the other end of the great oak dining-table, he got out his books again, put fresh wood on the fire, trimmed his lamp, and set himself down to a spell of real hard work. He went on without pause till about eleven o'clock, when he knocked off for a bit to fix his fire and lamp, and to make himself a cup of tea. He had always been a tea-drinker, and during his college life had sat late at work and had taken tea late. The rest was a great luxury to him, and he enjoyed it with a sense of delicious, voluptuous ease. The renewed fire leaped and sparkled, and threw quaint shadows through the great old room; and as he sipped his hot tea he revelled in the sense of isolation from his kind. Then it was that he began to notice for the first time what a noise the rats were making.

Surely, he thought, they cannot have been at it all the time I was reading. Had they been, I must have noticed it! Presently, when the noise increased, he satisfied himself that it was really new. It was evident that at first the rats had been frightened at the presence of a stranger, and the light of fire and lamp; but that as the time went on they had grown bolder and were disporting themselves as was their wont.

How busy they were! and hark to the strange noises! Up and down behind the old wainscot, over the ceiling and under the floor they raced, and gnawed, and scratched! Malcolmson smiled to himself as he recalled to mind the saying of Mrs Dempster, "Bogies is rats, and rats is bogies!" The tea began to have its effect of intellectual and nervous stimulus, he saw with joy another long spell of work to be done before the night was past, and in the sense of security which it gave him,

119

he allowed himself the luxury of a good look round the room. He took his lamp in one hand, and went all around, wondering that so quaint and beautiful an old house had been so long neglected. The carving of the oak on the panels of the wainscot was fine, and on and round the doors and windows it was beautiful and of rare merit. There were some old pictures on the walls, but they were coated so thick with dust and dirt that he could not distinguish any detail of them, though he held his lamp as high as he could over his head. Here and there as he went round he saw some crack or hole blocked for a moment by the face of a rat with its bright eyes glittering in the light, but in an instant it was gone, and a squeak and a scamper followed. The thing that most struck him, however, was the rope of the great alarm bell on the roof, which hung down in a corner of the room on the right-hand side of the fireplace. He pulled up close to the hearth a great high-backed carved oak chair, and sat down to his last cup of tea. When this was done he made up the fire, and went back to his work, sitting at the corner of the table, having the fire to his left. For a little while the rats disturbed him somewhat with their perpetual scampering, but he got accustomed to the noise as one does to the ticking of a clock or to the roar of moving water; and he became so immersed in his work that everything in the world, except the problem which he was trying to solve, passed away from him.

He suddenly looked up, his problem was still unsolved, and there was in the air that sense of the hour before the dawn, which is so dread to doubtful life. The noise of the rats had ceased. Indeed it seemed to him that it must have ceased but lately and that it was the sudden cessation which had disturbed him. The fire had fallen low, but still it threw out a deep red glow. As he looked he started in spite of his *sang froid*.

There on the great high-backed carved oak chair by the right side of the fireplace sat an enormous rat, steadily glaring at him with baleful eyes. He made a motion to it as though to

120

hunt it away, but it did not stir. The he made the motion of
throwing something. Still it did not stir, but showed its great
white teeth angrily, and its cruel eyes shone in the lamplight
with an added vindictiveness.

Malcolmson felt amazed, and seizing the poker from the
hearth ran at it to kill it. Before, however, he could strike it,
the rat, with a squeak that sounded like the concentration
of hate, jumped upon the floor, and, running up the rope of
the alarm bell, disappeared in the darkness beyond the range
of the green-shaded lamp. Instantly, strange to say, the noisy
scampering of the rats in the wainscot began again.

By this time Malcolmson's mind was quite off the
problem; and as a shrill cock-crow outside told him of the
approach of morning, he went to bed and to sleep.

He slept so sound that he was not even waked by Mrs
Dempster coming in to make up his room. It was only when
she had tidied up the place and got his breakfast ready and
tapped on the screen which closed in his bed that he woke.
He was a little tired still after his night's hard work, but a
strong cup of tea soon freshened him up and, taking his
book, he went out for his morning walk, bringing with him a
few sandwiches lest he should not care to return till dinner
time. He found a quiet walk between high elms some way
outside the town, and here he spent the greater part of the
day studying his Laplace. On his return he looked in to see
Mrs Witham and to thank her for her kindness. When she saw
him coming through the diamond-paned bay window of her
sanctum she came out to meet him and asked him in. She
looked at him searchingly and shook her head as she said:

"You must not overdo it, sir. You are paler this morning
than you should be. Too late hours and too hard work on the
brain isn't good for any man! But tell me, sir, how did you
pass the night? Well, I hope? But my heart! sir, I was glad
when Mrs Dempster told me this morning that you were all
right and sleeping sound when she went in."

"Oh, I was all right," he answered smiling, "the 'somethings' didn't worry me, as yet. Only the rats; and they had a circus, I tell you, all over the place. There was one wicked looking old devil that sat up on my own chair by the fire, and wouldn't go till I took the poker to him, and then he ran up the rope of the alarm bell and got to somewhere up the wall or the ceiling—I couldn't see where, it was so dark."

"Mercy on us," said Mrs Witham, "an old devil, and sitting on a chair by the fireside! Take care, sir! take care! There's many a true word spoken in jest."

"How do you mean? 'Pon my word I don't understand."

"An old devil! The old devil, perhaps. There, sir! You needn't laugh," for Malcolmson had broken into a hearty peal. "You young folks think it easy to laugh at things that makes older ones shudder. Never mind, sir! never mind! Please God, you'll laugh all the time. It's what I wish you myself!" and the good lady beamed all over in sympathy with his enjoyment, her fears gone for a moment.

"Oh, forgive me!" said Malcolmson presently. "Don't think me rude; but the idea was too much for me—that the old devil himself was on the chair last night!" And at the thought he laughed again. Then he went home to dinner.

This evening the scampering of the rats began earlier; indeed it had been going on before his arrival, and only ceased whilst his presence by its freshness disturbed them. After dinner he sat by the fire for a while and had a smoke; and then, having cleared his table, began to work as before. Tonight the rats disturbed him more than they had done on the previous night. How they scampered up and down and under and over! How they squeaked, and scratched, and gnawed! How they, getting bolder by degrees, came to the mouths of their holes and to the chinks and cracks and crannies in the wainscoting till their eyes shone like tiny lamps as the firelight rose and fell. But to him, now doubtless accustomed to them, their eyes were not wicked; only their playfulness touched him. Sometimes the boldest of them made sallies out on the floor or along the mouldings of the

122

wainscot. Now and again as they disturbed him Malcolmson made a sound to frighten them, smiting the table with his hand or giving a fierce "Hsh, hsh," so that they fled straightway to their holes. And so the early part of the night wore on; and despite the noise Malcolmson got more and more immersed in his work.

All at once he stopped, as on the previous night, being overcome by a sudden sense of silence. There was not the faintest sound of gnaw, or scratch, or squeak. The silence was as of the grave. He remembered the odd occurrence of the previous night, and instinctively he looked at the chair standing close by the fireside. And then a very odd sensation thrilled through him.

There, on the great old high-backed carved oak chair beside the fireplace, sat the same enormous rat, steadily glaring at him with baleful eyes.

Instinctively he took the nearest thing to his hand, a book of logarithms, and flung it at it. The book was badly aimed and the rat did not stir, so again the poker performance of the previous night was repeated; and again the rat, being closely pursued, fled up the rope of the alarm bell. Strangely too, the departure of this rat was instantly followed by the renewal of the noise made by the general rat community. On this occasion, as on the previous one, Malcolmson could not see at what part of the room the rat disappeared, for the green shade of his lamp left the upper part of the room in darkness, and the fire had burned low.

On looking at his watch he found it was close on midnight; and, not sorry for the *divertissement*, he made up his fire and made himself his nightly pot of tea. He had got through a good spell of work, and thought himself entitled to a cigarette; and so he sat on the great oak chair before the fire and enjoyed it. Whilst smoking he began to think that he would like to know where the rat disappeared to, for he had certain ideas for the morrow not entirely disconnected with a rat-trap. Accordingly he lit another lamp and placed it so that

123

it would shine well into the right-hand corner of the wall by the fireplace. Then he got all the books he had with him, and placed them handy to throw at the vermin. Finally he lifted the rope of the alarm bell and placed the end of it on the table, fixing the extreme end under the lamp. As he handled it he could not help noticing how pliable it was, especially for so strong a rope, and one not in use. You could hang a man with it, he thought to himself. When his preparations were made he looked around, and said complacently:

"There now, my friend, I think we shall learn something of you this time!" He began his work again, and though as before somewhat disturbed at first by the noise of the rats, soon lost himself in his propositions and problems.

Again he was called to his immediate surroundings suddenly. This time it might not have been the sudden silence only which took his attention; there was a slight movement of the rope, and the lamp moved. Without stirring, he looked to see if his pile of books was within range, and then cast his eye along the rope. As he looked he saw the great rat drop from the rope on the oak armchair and sit there glaring at him. He raised a book in his right hand, and taking careful aim, flung it at the rat. The latter, with a quick movement, sprang aside and dodged the missile. He then took another book, and a third, and flung them one after another at the rat, but each time unsuccessfully. At last, as he stood with a book poised in his hand to throw, the rat squeaked and seemed afraid. This made Malcolmson more than ever eager to strike, and the book flew and struck the rat a resounding blow. It gave a terrified squeak, and turning on his pursuer a look of terrible malevolence, ran up the chair-back and made a great jump to the rope of the alarm bell and ran up it like lightning. The lamp rocked under the sudden strain, but it was a heavy one and did not topple over. Malcolmson kept his eyes on the rat, and saw it by the light of the second lamp leap to a moulding of the wainscot and disappear through a hole in one of the great pictures which hung on the wall, obscured and invisible through its coating of dirt and dust.

"I shall look up my friend's habitation in the morning," said the student, as he went over to collect his books. "The third picture from the fireplace; I shall not forget." He picked up the books one by one, commenting on them as he lifted them. *"Conic Sections* he does not mind, nor *Cycloidal Oscillations*, nor the *Principia*, nor *Quaternions*, nor *Thermodynamics*. Now for the book that fetched him!" Malcolmson took it up and looked at it. As he did so he started, and a sudden pallor overspread his face. He looked round uneasily and shivered slightly, as he murmured to himself:

"The Bible my mother gave me! What an odd coincidence." He sat down to work again, and the rats in the wainscot renewed their gambols. They did not disturb him, however; somehow their presence gave him a sense of companionship. But he could not attend to his work, and after striving to master the subject on which he was engaged gave it up in despair, and went to bed as the first streak of dawn stole in through the eastern window.

He slept heavily but uneasily, and dreamed much; and when Mrs Dempster woke him late in the morning he seemed ill at ease, and for a few minutes did not seem to realize exactly where he was. His first request rather surprised the servant.

"Mrs Dempster, when I am out today I wish you would get the steps and dust or wash those pictures—specially that one the third from the fireplace—I want to see what they are."

Late in the afternoon Malcolmson worked at his books in the shaded walk, and the cheerfulness of the previous day came back to him as the day wore on, and he found that his reading was progressing well. He had worked out to a satisfactory conclusion all the problems which had as yet baffled him, and it was in a state of jubilation that he paid a visit to Mrs Witham at The Good Traveller. He found a stranger in the cosy sitting-room with the landlady, who was introduced to him as Dr Thornhill. She was not at ease, and

125

this, combined with the Doctor's plunging at once into a series of questions, made Malcolmson come to the conclusion that his presence was not an accident, so without preliminary he said:

"Dr Thornhill, I shall with pleasure answer you any question you may choose to ask me if you will answer me one question first."

The Doctor seemed surprised, but he smiled and answered at once, "Done! What is it?"

"Did Mrs Witham ask you to come here and see me and advise me?"

Dr Thornhill for a moment was taken aback, and Mrs Witham got fiery red and turned away; but the Doctor was a frank and ready man, and he answered at once and openly.

"She did: but she didn't intend you to know it. I suppose it was my clumsy haste that made you suspect. She told me that she did not like the idea of your being in that house all by yourself, and that she thought you took too much strong tea. In fact, she wants me to advise you if possible to give up the tea and the very late hours. I was a keen student in my time, so I suppose I may take the liberty of a college man, and without offence, advise you not quite as a stranger."

Malcolmson with a bright smile held out his hand. "Shake! as they say in America," he said. "I must thank you for your kindness and Mrs Witham too, and your kindness deserves a return on my part. I promise to take no more strong tea—no tea at all till you let me—and I shall go to bed tonight at one o'clock at latest. Will that do?"

"Capital," said the Doctor. "Now tell us all that you noticed in the old house," and so Malcolmson then and there told in minute detail all that had happened in the last two nights. He was interrupted every now and then by some exclamation from Mrs Witham, till finally when he told of the episode of the Bible the landlady's pent-up emotions found vent in a shriek; and it was not till a stiff glass of brandy and water had been administered that she grew

126

composed again. Dr Thornhill listened with a face of growing gravity, and when the narrative was complete and Mrs Witham had been restored he asked:

"The rat always went up the rope of the alarm bell?"

"Always."

"I suppose you know," said the Doctor after a pause, "what the rope is?"

"No!"

"It is," said the Doctor slowly, "the very rope which the hangman used for all the victims of the Judge's judicial rancour!" Here he was interrupted by another scream from Mrs Witham, and steps had to be taken for her recovery. Malcolmson having looked at his watch, and found that it was close to his dinner hour, had gone home before her complete recovery.

When Mrs Witham was herself again she almost assailed the Doctor with angry questions as to what he meant by putting such horrible ideas into the poor young man's mind. "He has quite enough there already to upset him," she added. Dr Thornhill replied:

"My dear madam, I had a distinct purpose in it! I wanted to draw his attention to the bell rope, and to fix it there. It may be that he is in a highly overwrought state, and has been studying too much, although I am bound to say that he seems as sound and healthy a young man, mentally and bodily, as ever I saw—but then the rats—and that suggestion of the devil." The Doctor shook his head and went on. "I would have offered to go and stay the first night with him but that I felt sure it would have been a cause of offence. He may get in the night some strange fright or hallucination; and if he does I want him to pull that rope. All alone as he is it will give us warning, and we may reach him in time to be of service. I shall be sitting up pretty late tonight and shall keep my ears open. Do not be alarmed if Benchurch gets a surprise before morning."

"Oh, Doctor, what do you mean? What do you mean?"

127

"I mean this; that possibly—nay, more probably—we shall hear the great alarm bell from the Judge's House tonight," and the Doctor made about as effective an exit as could be thought of.

When Malcolmson arrived home he found that it was a little after his usual time, and Mrs Dempster had gone away—the rules of Greenhow's Charity were not to be neglected. He was glad to see that the place was bright and tidy with a cheerful fire and a well-trimmed lamp. The evening was colder than might have been expected in April, and a heavy wind was blowing with such rapidly-increasing strength that there was every promise of a storm during the night. For a few minutes after his entrance the noise of the rats ceased; but so soon as they became accustomed to his presence they began again. He was glad to hear them, for he felt once more the feeling of companionship in their noise, and his mind ran back to the strange fact that they only ceased to manifest themselves when that other—the great rat with the baleful eyes—came upon the scene. The reading-lamp only was lit and its green shade kept the ceiling and the upper part of the room in darkness, so that the cheerful light from the hearth spreading over the floor and shining on the white cloth laid over the end of the table was warm and cheery. Malcolmson sat down to his dinner with a good appetite and a buoyant spirit. After his dinner and a cigarette he sat steadily down to work, determined not to let anything disturb him, for he remembered his promise to the Doctor, and made up his mind to make the best of the time at his disposal.

For an hour or so he worked all right, and then his thoughts began to wander from his books. The actual circumstances around him, the calls on his physical attention, and his nervous susceptibility were not to be denied. By this time the wind had become a gale, and the gale a storm. The old house, solid though it was, seemed to shake to its foundations, and the storm roared and raged through its many chimneys and its queer old gables, producing strange, unearthly sounds in the empty rooms and corridors. Even the great alarm bell on the roof must have felt the force of the wind, for the rope rose and fell slightly, as though the bell were moved a little from time to time, and the limber rope fell on the oak floor with a hard and hollow sound.

As Malcolmson listened to it he bethought himself of the Doctor's words: "It is the very rope which the hangman used for all the victims of the Judge's judicial rancour," and he went over to the corner of the fireplace and took it in his hand to look at it. There seemed a sort of deadly interest in it, and as he stood there he lost himself for a moment in speculation as to who these victims were, and the grim wish of the Judge to have such a ghastly relic ever under his eyes. As he stood there the swaying of the bell on the roof still lifted the rope now and again; but presently there came a new sensation—a sort of tremor in the rope, as though something was moving along it.

Looking up instinctively Malcolmson saw the great rat coming slowly down towards him, glaring at him steadily. He dropped the rope and started back with a muttered curse, and the rat, turning, ran up the rope again and disappeared, and at the same instant Malcolmson became conscious that the noise of the rats, which had ceased for a while, began again.

All this set him thinking, and it occurred to him that he had not investigated the lair of the rat or looked at the pictures, as he had intended. He lit the other lamp without the shade, and, holding it up went and stood opposite the third picture from the fireplace on the right-hand side where he had seen the rat disappear on the previous night.

At the first glance he started back so suddenly that he almost dropped the lamp, and a deadly pallor over-spread his face. His knees shook, and heavy drops of sweat came on his forehead, and he trembled like an aspen. But he was young and plucky, and pulled himself together, and after the pause of a few seconds stepped forward again, raised the lamp, and examined the picture which had been dusted and washed, and now stood out clearly.

It was of a judge dressed in his robes of scarlet and ermine. His face was strong and merciless, evil, crafty, and vindictive, with a sensual mouth, hooked nose of ruddy colour, and shaped like the beak of a bird of prey. The rest of the face was of a cadaverous colour. The eyes were of peculiar brilliance and with a terribly malignant expression. As he looked at them, Malcolmson grew cold, for he saw there the very counterpart of the eyes of the great rat. The lamp almost fell from his hand, he saw the rat with its baleful eyes peering out through the hole in the corner of the picture, and noted the sudden cessation of the noise of the other rats. However, he pulled himself together, and went on with his examination of the picture.

The Judge was seated in a great high-backed carved oak chair, on the right-hand side of a great stone fireplace where, in the corner, a rope hung down from the ceiling, its end lying coiled on the floor. With a feeling of something like horror, Malcolmson recognized the scene of the room as it stood, and gazed around him in an awestruck manner as though he expected to find some strange presence behind him. Then he looked over to the corner of the fireplace—and with a loud cry he let the lamp fall from his hand.

There, in the Judge's arm-chair, with the rope hanging behind, sat the rat with the Judge's baleful eyes, now intensified and with a fiendish leer. Save for the howling of the storm without there was silence.

The fallen lamp recalled Malcolmson to himself. Fortunately it was of metal, and so the oil was not spilt. However, the practical need of attending to it settled at once his nervous apprehensions. When he had turned it out, he wiped his brow and thought for a moment.

"This will not do," he said to himself. "If I go on like this I shall become a crazy fool. This must stop! I promised the

130

Doctor I would not take tea. Faith, he was pretty right! My nerves must have been getting into a queer state. Funny I did not notice it. I never felt better in my life. However, it is all right now, and I shall not be such a fool again."

Then he mixed himself a good stiff glass of brandy and water and resolutely sat down to his work.

It was nearly an hour when he looked up from his book, disturbed by the sudden stillness. Without, the wind howled and roared louder than ever, and the rain drove in sheets against the windows, beating like hail on the glass; but within there was no sound whatever save the echo of the wind as it roared in the great chimney, and now and then a hiss as a few raindrops found their way down the chimney in a lull of the storm. The fire had fallen low and had ceased to flame, though it threw out a red glow. Malcolmson listened attentively, and presently heard a thin, squeaking noise, very faint. It came from the corner of the room where the rope hung down, and he thought it was the creaking of the rope on the floor as the swaying of the bell raised and lowered it. Looking up, however, he saw in the dim light the great rat clinging to the rope and gnawing it. The rope was already nearly gnawed through—he could see the lighter colour where the strands were laid bare. As he looked the job was completed, and the severed end of the rope fell clattering on the oaken floor, whilst for an instant the great rat remained like a knob or tassel at the end of the rope, which now began to sway to and fro. Malcolmson felt for a moment another pang of terror at the thought that now the possibility of calling the outer world to his assistance was cut off, but an intense anger took its place, and seizing the book he was reading he hurled it at the rat. The blow was well aimed, but before the missile could reach him the rat dropped off and struck the floor with a soft thud. Malcolmson instantly rushed over towards him, but it darted away and disappeared in the darkness of the shadows of the room. Malcolmson felt that his work was over for the night, and determined then

131

and there to vary the monotony of the proceedings by a hunt for the rat, and took off the green shade of the lamp so as to ensure a wider spreading light. As he did so the gloom of the upper part of the room was relieved, and in the new flood of light, great by comparison with the previous darkness, the pictures on the wall stood out boldly. From where he stood, Malcolmson saw right opposite to him the third picture on the wall from the right of the fireplace. He rubbed his eyes in surprise, and then a great fear began to come upon him.

In the centre of the picture was a great irregular patch of brown canvas, as fresh as when it was stretched on the frame. The background was as before, with chair and chimney-corner and rope, but the figure of the Judge had disappeared.

Malcolmson, almost in a chill of horror, turned slowly round, and then he began to shake and tremble like a man in a palsy. His strength seemed to have left him, and he was incapable of action or movement, hardly even of thought. He could only see and hear.

There, on the great high-backed carved oak chair sat the Judge in his robes of scarlet and ermine, with his baleful eyes glaring vindictively, and a smile of triumph on the resolute, cruel mouth, as he lifted with his hands a *black cap*. Malcolmson felt as if the blood was running from his heart, as one does in moments of prolonged suspense. There was a singing in his ears. Without, he could hear the roar and howl of the tempest, and through it, swept on the storm, came the striking of midnight by the great chimes in the market place. He stood, for a space of time that seemed to him endless, still as a statue, and with wide-open, horror-struck eyes, breathless. As the clock struck, so the smile of triumph on the Judge's face intensified, and at the last stroke of midnight he placed the black cap on his head.

Slowly and deliberately the Judge rose from his chair and picked up the piece of the rope of the alarm bell which lay on the floor, drew it through his hands as if he enjoyed its touch, and then deliberately began to knot one end of it,

132

fashioning it into a noose. This he tightened and tested with his foot, pulling hard at it till he was satisfied and then making a running noose of it, which he held in his hand. Then he began to move along the table on the opposite side to Malcolmson keeping his eyes on him until he had passed him, when with a quick movement he stood in front of the door. Malcolmson then began to feel that he was trapped, and tried to think of what he should do. There was some fascination in the Judge's eyes, which he never took off him, and he had, perforce, to look. He saw the Judge approach— still keeping between him and the door—and raise the noose and throw it towards him as if to entangle him. With a great effort he made a quick movement to one side, and saw the rope fall beside him, and heard it strike the oaken floor. Again the Judge raised the noose and tried to ensnare him, ever keeping his baleful eyes fixed on him, and each time by a mighty effort the student just managed to evade it. So this went on for many times, the Judge seeming never discouraged nor discomposed at failure, but playing as a cat does with a mouse. At last in despair, which had reached its climax, Malcolmson cast a quick glance round him. The lamp seemed to have blazed up, and there was a fairly good light in the room. At the many rat-holes and in the chinks and crannies of the wainscot he saw the rats' eyes; and this aspect, that was purely physical, gave him a gleam of comfort. He looked around and saw that the rope of the great alarm bell was laden with rats. Every inch of it was covered with them, and more and more were pouring through the small circular hole in the ceiling whence it emerged, so that with their weight the bell was beginning to sway.

Hark! It had swayed till the clapper had touched the bell. The sound was but a tiny one, but the bell was only beginning to sway, and it would increase.

At the sound the Judge, who had been keeping his eyes fixed on Malcolmson, looked up, and a scowl of diabolical anger overspread his face. His eyes fairly glowed like hot

133

coals, and he stamped his foot with a sound that seemed to make the house shake. A dreadful peal of thunder broke overhead as he raised the rope again, whilst the rats kept running up and down the rope as though working against time. This time, instead of throwing it, he drew close to his victim, and held open the noose as he approached. As he came closer there seemed something paralysing in his very presence, and Malcolmson stood rigid as a corpse. He felt the Judge's icy fingers touch his throat as he adjusted the rope. The noose tightened—tightened. Then the Judge, taking the rigid form of the student in his arms, carried him over and placed him standing in the oak chair, and stepping up beside him, put his hand up and caught the end of the swaying rope of the alarm bell. As he raised his hand the rats fled squeaking, and disappeared through the hole in the ceiling. Taking the end of the noose which was round Malcolmson's neck he tied it to the hanging-bell rope, and then descending pulled away the chair.

When the alarm bell of the Judge's House began to sound a crowd soon assembled. Lights and torches of various kinds appeared, and soon a silent crowd was hurrying to the spot. They knocked loudly at the door, but there was no reply. Then they burst in the door, and poured into the great dining-room, the Doctor at the head.

There at the end of the rope of the great alarm bell hung the body of the student, and on the face of the Judge in the picture was a malignant smile.

8
The Tall Woman
Rosemary Timperley

It was after the tall woman had been following her for several days that she reported the matter to the police. She walked through the falling snow to the police station, pushed open the big swing doors, explained briefly to a young constable at a desk, then was shown into an office where a sergeant interviewed her.

First he asked for particulars about herself: name, address, age, occupation. When he heard that she was a widow of nearly sixty, living alone and not doing a job, virtually friendless and without living relatives, he gave her a cautious look.

"I know what you're thinking," she said, looking with fear at the snowflakes fluttering against the windowpanes. "You're thinking that I'm a neurotic woman going round the bend through being alone too much. It's true that I'm alone a lot. I even talk to myself. What's the harm in that? People are usually only talking to themselves even when there's someone else there. But I've never suffered from hallucinations or delusions of persecution. I know for a fact that I *am* being followed."

135

"Can you describe this person who follows you, madam?"

"She's a very tall woman, in her thirties at a guess. She has brown hair, like the colour of dirty snow. It hangs to her shoulders like muddy rain. She has staring eyes and a colourless face. Wherever I go, either I see her standing looking at me or, if I look behind me, I see her following. Her expression is—predatory."

The man cleared his throat and gave a brief sigh. She could almost see the balloon of his thought, as in a cartoon: *Another nut!*

"Once I plucked up the courage to stop and wait for her to overtake me, but she stopped too."

"Didn't you then walk back and ask what she wanted?"

"No. I was too frightened."

"Madam, if this lady lives in the neighbourhood, it's quite natural that you should often see her around. I expect she merely goes shopping at the same times as yourself."

"No. I deliberately go out at different times, to avoid her, but she's always there."

"How is she dressed?"

"Always the same. She wears a rather old-fashioned brown suit. Muddy brown, like her hair. The shoulders have a padded look, like a man's suit. She'd be nondescript in appearance if it weren't for her height. She's too tall. I read once that extra-tall people have criminal tendencies. She's dangerous. I know it."

"Mmmm. And what exactly did you expect us to do?"

"Protect me from her, of course. Isn't that what the police are for?"

"But as far as I can make out, she hasn't done you any harm. If she threatened or assaulted you—"

"She threatens me all the time, by being there."

"With a nervous lady like you, it's possible to imagine such things."

"I am not a 'nervous lady'. I am supremely self-controlled. If you knew what I've had to control, all my life—" She

136

broke off. The police are just as stupid as they ever were, she thought. They believed me when I lied and now they don't believe me when I'm telling the truth.

"I don't imagine the tall woman," she said. "She is real and she follows me. Can't you get one of your men to keep an eye on me? Then if anything did happen—"

"We'll keep our eyes open," he said soothingly, "but you must understand we can't spare you a full time bodyguard. That's only done in exceptional circumstances."

"These are exceptional circumstances. I don't know why she hates me, but she's after my blood—after my body, my flesh, my bones. She followed me here today."

"She hasn't followed you inside."

"So far she's never followed me indoors. One day she will. I shall be helpless. She's so tall."

"You're quite a tall lady yourself."

"She'll be waiting outside," she said. "In the snow. It was when the season of snow began that she started to follow me. It provides cover for her."

The sergeant said matter-of-factly, "I suggest that you go to the door, see if she's there, and come back and tell me. If she is, then I'll go and sort her out. Okay?"

"Very well."

She left his office, crossed the corridor to the swing doors, looked through the glass—and there was the tall woman, standing in the snow, staring at her.

Returning to the office, she said: "Yes. She's there."

"All right, madam. Wait here." He went to the door and looked out. Seeing no one, he went right outside and glanced up and down the street. There were not many people about. The evening rush hour had not started and the bad weather had kept most of the shopping-women indoors. There were two women at the bus-stop but both were short and plump. He shook his head a little and returned to the "nut" in his office. Persecution mania was a dodgy thing. The victims always *knew* they were right. They didn't seem to need concrete evidence.

"I don't know who you saw, madam, but there's no one of that description there now."

"She's cunning!"

"Do you know what I think you ought to do? Go and see your doctor. Registered with a G.P., are you?"

"Yes. Doctor Ganton. But I'm not ill."

"When people worry a lot and get run down, they can be iller than they know. You go and tell Doctor Ganton the whole story."

"You think I'm making it up. Forgive me for having wasted your time." With some dignity, she walked out into the snow. She wished she hadn't asked for help now. Going to the police had been a last resort. Now, having used it up, she felt even more helpless than before.

She glanced behind her. The tall woman was following. More than that. She was following at a shorter distance than before. Insidiously, she was catching up.

The policeman's words of advice returned to her. Perhaps a word with Doctor Ganton would be a good idea after all. She certainly felt very shaky and upset. Tranquillizers might help. When in danger, one needed to keep calm.

It was early evening when she reached Doctor Ganton's surgery. As she pushed open his gate, she looked back. The woman had stopped when she did and was standing, staring. She stared back. Only the snowflakes veiled their eyes from each other. She shivered as old memories stirred, then turned and dived into the warmth of the doctor's house.

She sat in the waiting-room. Each time the door opened and new patients arrived, she looked up fearfully in case the woman came in. For one day the woman *would* come in—right in—and then ... But it didn't happen. While the other patients eyed her curiously, she crossed to the window and peeped through the white net curtain. She saw the tall woman standing at the gate. Their eyes met through the snow.

138

At last it was her turn to go into the doctor's room. Cool, young, dark-eyed, Doctor Ganton was at his desk. After the polite preliminaries, he asked: "What can I do for you?"

"I'm being followed, Doctor." She filled in the details as she had done at the police station, and concluded: "The police are no use. Either they don't believe a word I say, or they don't want to."

"This woman," said Doctor Ganton, "does she remind you of anyone you know, or used to know?"

"That's hard to answer. She does and she doesn't. I do feel as if I've seen her before, but I can't pin it down. I've pictured all the people I've ever known—even people who serve in shops or work on buses—who might have got it in for me for some reason I never knew about, but it's no use. I can't link her up with anyone."

"So as far as you know she's a complete stranger."

"A complete stranger. And she's out there now, waiting for me."

He smiled. "That simplifies things. Go and fetch her in. Say I'd like a word with her."

"No! I can't fetch her in! I won't!"

He rose purposefully. In a trice he was out of the room and at the front door. She waited. Silence. Then she heard him coming back and talking to someone. She ran over to the far side of the room and stood against the wall. Then she heard him say, "Right, Mrs Balcon, I'll be seeing you later. Bit of a queue tonight, I'm afraid," and he was back in the surgery.

"No sign of your tall woman," he said.

"Who was—Mrs Balcon?"

"Patient arriving." He lowered his voice: "Five feet tall and dressed in red. Come and sit down again. How are you sleeping?"

"Not very well."

"Lack of sleep can make one 'see things'. Did you know that?" He was writing on his prescription pad. "Pilots, night

139

nurses, even we doctors—when we've been without sleep for some time, visions appear before our eyes. Now, I want you to take these tablets, three times a day. The chemist's shop at the top of the hill stays open late tonight, so you can take this prescription there straight away. That'll ensure you get a good night's rest. Come back and see me in a week or so and tell me how you're getting on."

"Thank you."

As she left, she heard him say: "Next, please. Good evening, Mr Brent. Sorry to have kept you waiting."

When she stepped outside, she found that the world was still white but the snow was no longer falling. And the tall woman had gone. Where was she? Instead of feeling relieved, she felt more uneasy than ever. At least, when she'd been following, she'd known where the creature *was*.

She walked to the chemist's shop in the white night and collected her tablets. It took some time as most of the doctor's patients came straight from the surgery to the shop, the queue transferring itself piecemeal from one place to the next. Only when she reached the house where she lived did the snow begin to fall again. As she fitted her key into the front door, she looked behind her.

The tall woman was standing at the gate, closer to her than ever before. She almost fell into the house, slamming the door behind her, then leaning against it, strangely breathless.

Recovering herself, she began to climb the stairs to her first-floor bed-sitter.

"Wait a minute, dear!" Mrs Bates, her landlady, had come out of the ground-floor flat. "You had a visitor while you were out," she said.

"Me? I don't have visitors."

"It was you she wanted. Tall lady in brown. She said she'd be back."

"Did she give her name?"

"No. I didn't ask. I thought you'd know. She's a relation, is she?"

"I have no relations."

"Oh, silly of me. I only guessed she might be because she looked so like you. At first I thought it *was* you. But she was younger. Might have been your daughter, if you had one. Are you all right, dear?"

"I'm not very well. I've been to the doctor."

"Oh, I am sorry. This weather's enough to make anyone seedy. All this snow makes me feel quite funny in the head."

"Yes."

"I hope you'll soon feel better."

"Thank you, Mrs Bates."

"I don't expect your visitor will come again tonight."

But, when she reached her room and looked out of the window, she saw her "visitor" still standing outside. Mrs Bates's words echoed in her head: *Might have been your daughter, if you had one.* Fragments of sound tossed back and forth in a cave of ice.

Shivering, she lit the gas-fire and crouched before it. "I have no daughter," she whispered to the whispering gas.

Indeed she had never thought of the baby as a daughter. Only as a baby. As *it*. She hadn't wanted it in the first place. When told she was going to have it, she'd wanted to get rid of it, but her husband prevented her. So she'd had to wait for it to come. It wasn't like waiting for a person to come. A person came from outside. *It* was coming from inside. It gave her hell when it actually arrived, a long drawn out agony of red ice and black fire. She hated it on sight yet had to pretend to love it, because an unloving mother was a disgrace to humanity. No one, least of all her husband, must know how she really felt. She hadn't realized before how excellent were her powers of acting and self-control. She put on the performance of her life, and it split her in two: there was the sweet, loving mother, always on show, and the real cold woman gasping unseen in dark depths of guilt and misery.

And the baby had sensed it. It had screamed itself hoarse in her presence. It knew that it was unloved by its mother

141

even though no one else knew. People had suspected that there might be something wrong with the baby because of the way it behaved. She had known that the baby was right and it was herself who had something wrong.

Impersonally, she could be sorry for it. She pitied it for being born. She kept wishing it could be put out of its misery.

Wishing is dangerous stuff. It can lead to black daydream. She daydreamed of life without the baby, life as it had been before the baby was born, and as it could be again if the baby were to vanish. Peace would return and freedom. Books to read, theatres to visit, friends to entertain, without *it* screaming in the background, or in the foreground, with everyone drooling over it and making goo-goo noises to it. It had ruined everything, and all the time she had to smile and smile and do some goo-gooing herself, so as to seem a "natural mother". Her husband had positively grovelled to it. She couldn't see what he saw in it. It gave nothing. It only took, and yelled. If only it would vanish. But how did one make a baby vanish?

Came the day of the snow. It fell so thickly that trains from town were delayed for hours. Her husband telephoned from work to say that he wouldn't be home till God knows when. So there was just the white evening, the house among the fields, herself, and *it*.

It screamed and screamed and screamed, as if it knew what was coming. Yet—if it had kept quiet, would she have done what she did? She struck it. First time she'd ever done that. And it stopped screaming and stared into her eyes. She was never quite sure whether she saw in its eyes real human hatred, or a reflection of her own hatred.

She picked it up and carried it across the fields. She saw her breath in the air, and as she walked her breath turned from a pale cloud to a darker cloud and then seemed to form little black shapes, like imps dancing against the snow.

She had come to a snow-filled ditch protected by a

142

snow-heavy hedge. She plunged *it* into the cold bed. Its eyes had stared with loathing and anger more than fear. She had pressed snow over its eyes, then snow in its mouth.

In beautiful silence she had walked back to the house. Her breath still formed those tiny black impish figures each time she exhaled. They dropped like fancy jet jigsaw pieces on to the white ground and danced ahead of her. As she moved, the falling snow filled in her footprints so that the journey might never have been made.

The actress in her kept up some sort of pretence when she entered the house. She behaved as if there were hidden cameras and bugging devices all around, and "put the baby to bed". Then she went to bed herself.

And she felt so wonderfully free!

But the show must go on. When her husband returned, very late indeed, he came into the bedroom and asked if she'd got the baby in bed with her. No, she said, all innocent surprise. Why? Because he'd gone to say goodnight and it wasn't in its cot. She recalled that she had almost said: "Perhaps it's gone for a walk," then suppressed the frivolous remark. She must keep up the act.

The act proved easy in the days to follow. There was tremendous upheaval, panic and search—police, neighbours, reporters, telephone calls, newspaper headlines, even television coverage. A picture of *it* on the screen: *Have you seen this child?*

That was memorable: its eyes had looked at her from the screen and had seemed to blink.

But she played her part of the desperately anguished mother very well. She *was* desperately anguished. She was terrified of being found out. She had to keep reminding herself that she was the only person who knew for a fact that it was dead. She had only to let one careless word slip and her crime might be revealed.

It never was revealed. Her husband, the police and everyone else drew the final conclusion that the child had been stolen. Fortunately for her, there had been quite an outbreak of baby-stealing in the area. Demented women, as if infected by each other, had been taking babies from prams or cots and, if they were caught, being unable to explain why they had done such a thing—nor had they seen anything really wrong in doing it. She felt she understood them better than most. They were like her, but at the opposite end of the scale. She had hated being with a baby, and they hated being without one. There comes a moment of just handing over the soul to the Devil and grabbing the heart's desire.

She had buried it in the snow to retrieve past pleasures and get peace and quiet. She had made her wish come true by making the baby vanish. But, as in all the best fairy-stories, wishes which come true do so with a twist in the tail. For she had not retrieved either pleasure or peace and quiet.

Her husband, grief-stricken, had withdrawn from her. He had buried himself in his work as stiflingly as his child had been buried in snow. There was no pleasure in his company. Nor was it quiet. For she kept hearing the baby scream. And she didn't dare tell anyone about that for common sense told her that the noise must be inside her own head although it seemed to come from outside. She did not want to be thought mad when she knew she wasn't. In fact, she was amazed by the firmness of her sanity. Wonderful to keep so sane after all she'd been through, with never a confidante, never a chance to relax.

But as the years passed the screaming faded and she adapted to the treadmill of the cold marriage, the domestic, routined, pedestrian existence. It was simply a matter of putting one foot in front of the other.

Then her husband died and she was quite alone. By that time the past seemed unreal, as if it had all happened to someone else, or as if it had been a nightmare and had never happened at all. Without a past or a future, she had become an empty vessel, a vacuum at the mercy of any influence that might come her way. Her only remaining emotion now was

144

fear of the unknown, and snow always increased that fear. And now fear stalked her footsteps in the snow, followed her in the form of the tall woman, the "visitor" at the gate. *Might have been your daughter, if you had one.*

Suddenly an idea came to her. It was not a new idea. She had thought of it sometimes in the past, but brushed it aside as ridiculous. It was this: Just suppose that *it* had not died in the snow. Suppose someone had passed that way immediately after she'd left, had found it, given it a name, educated it, dressed it—and sent it out into the world. And then suppose *it*, fully adult now, had found out . . .

Suppose it was now the tall woman, and it knew what she had done. Suppose the tall woman really was her daughter! *She's a relation, is she? I only guessed she might be because she looked so like you. At first I thought it was you. But she was younger. Might have been your daughter . . .*

She got up from the fire and looked at herself in the mirror above the mantlepiece. The mirror hung high because she was such a tall woman. She studied her reflected face and for a moment seemed to be staring at the woman who followed her, the woman of thirty or so, in the old-fashioned clothes. The colouring was different. Her hair was grey, the other's was brown. Her suit was grey, the other's was brown. Her eyes were grey, the other's were indefinable. But the shape and pallor of her face was the same as the other's face. That was why the tall woman had seemed familiar. She had reminded her of herself at that age.

She looked out of the window again. The tall woman was standing halfway up the path and staring up at her. How real and solid she was. This was no vision caused by sleepless nights. This was *it*, grown-up and vengeful!

A flare of hate warmed her. And she was relieved in a curious way. For although with both the police and the doctor she had stressed that she was not imagining things, a doubt had lurked in her secret mind: a notion that perhaps her genuine guilt, concealed perfectly for a lifetime, had somehow got out of herself and taken on tangible form, turning into an ever-present persecutor when the snow fell. That fear had been twice reinforced when policeman and doctor had failed to see the woman, but Mrs Bates had seen her all right!

Now that she knew what she was up against, she would be brave—like that other time when she'd walked across the fields in the snow and her black breath had been a devils' dance. She would go down to the front door, and invite the tall woman in. She would offer her some coffee—and put something in it. She had always kept "something" in case of being found out and needing the release of suicide. But it wasn't she who was going to die. *It* was.

The tall woman took a step forward on the path.

She drew back from the window, heart pounding.

"Afraid of your own daughter?" she mocked herself.

The self-taunt spurred her on and she moved to the door, intending to go right down there and let the woman in. But, as she moved, she glimpsed another movement out of the corner of her eye and turned to look at the window again.

The tall woman was staring in.

"Damned cheek!" she cried. "Daughter or no daughter, you have no right to come peering through my window!"

She took a step towards the window, then stopped—petrified—for this was a *first floor* window. No woman, however tall, was as tall as that.

The face came nearer. She stared long and terribly into *its* eyes. Blackness fell over her. And in that icy darkness, she felt as if unseen hands were thrusting her down deeply into a ditch of deadly snow.

"You're looking better today, I must say," Mrs Bates commented next morning as her lodger came down the stairs. "Touched your hair up, have you, dear? And I like your brown suit. You look years younger—more like your visitor

146

than ever. Any message for her if she comes back?"

"I'm here already," was the cool reply, which didn't mean much to Mrs Bates, but then lodgers were always a funny lot.

A Matter of Timing
Gladys Greenaway

I was later than usual that evening for it had been one of those days in which everything happened. I keep a little junk shop. Junk shop it is, advisedly. A few antiques but mainly odds and ends, some useful, some just pretty.

I had been to a sale some miles away and bought a lot of small stuff which I brought away with me, among it the carved head of an old man.

Alice, my assistant, is a wonderful saleswoman. A quiet, middle-aged woman with friendly blue eyes. She has a real feeling for old things but no idea of value, so everything must be marked carefully. She lives over the shop which is a great asset.

I priced everything I had bought apart from the head. That I looked at carefully but I hadn't an idea of its value for it had been in amongst a lot of junk. It fascinated me. It was nut-brown and beautifully carved. There was a look of ageless wisdom in the hollow cheeks and deepset eyes. It was one of those cases of buying to sell and then feeling I couldn't sell it. Wrapping it in a piece of cloth I put it on the floor behind the driving seat. George would like it.

148

George and I live about five miles out of our little market town in a charming old cottage. George is a naturalist and I have a feeling that local people think he leads a lazy, easy-going life, but the opposite is the case. He works extremely hard lecturing and writing, is the most gentle creature and with a wonderful sense of fun.

Life has been good to us and we enjoy each other's company apart from loving each other.

Our cottage is on a side road which leads to Miller's farm. Beyond the farm the road is little more than a cart track to the nearest village and is seldom used by those who value their cars, although it is a short cut. In the five years we had lived there I had never met another car in the evening.

I turned into our road. It was quite dark and my headlights were full on. It is a long road and narrow, not much more than a lane. Halfway to the cottage there is a sharp bend to the left. I saw the lights before I reached the bend but it was too late. The car came on, headlights glaring. I jammed on the brakes and swung the wheel but it was useless. There was a terrific crash, I heard the shattering of glass and I knew no more until I heard a man's voice saying, "This one's dead. Call an ambulance and the police. I'll have a look in the other car."

I knew the voice. It was Harry Jones who lives just round on the other side of the bend. Was I dead? I couldn't move but I was in no pain. Was this death in which there was no pain, no movement, just thoughts? Then I knew nothing.

The nothingness didn't last. I began to think again and found I could lift my head and move my limbs. I wasn't hurt! The car was slewed round to the right. I could see ahead clearly. The windscreen wasn't even cracked and there was no sign of another car. Slowly I pulled myself together. I was shaking from head to foot but nothing else. I released my safety belt and got out. There was nothing wrong, no glass on the road, not the slightest damage.

Getting back in I started the engine and straightened the

car out. Then I drove round the corner and stopped the engine. I was still shaking and bewildered. What had happened? I had seen the other car and the headlights, felt the impact, heard the shattering of glass, and yet there was nothing wrong. I had heard Harry Jones's voice so distinctly. Had I blacked out and dreamt the whole thing? Looking at my watch I knew the incident had taken no longer than a few minutes.

I drove the rest of the way slowly and carefully. I put the car in the garage and went in the back door. George was in the kitchen preparing supper. It was an unwritten agreement that when I went to a sale he did the cooking. He looked up from the sink.

"What's wrong? You're as white as a ghost."

"I'm all right. A bit tired, that's all."

"Go and sit down. I'll bring you a drink."

I didn't want a drink. What I wanted was to throw myself into George's arms and tell him what had happened but somehow I couldn't. In the comfortable living-room with the softly shaded lights it all seemed completely mad. George would think I was crazy.

I was still shaking but with a drink inside me and then supper on a tray I not only felt better but I was also convinced I had fallen asleep at the wheel but had managed to stop the car before I had an accident. The rest had been one of those dreams that take place in seconds. Probably the subconscious telling me what could happen if I drove fast when tired. I was tired, far more tired than I ever remembered being before. Not ordinary tiredness which comes after a hard day's work, but complete exhaustion. I had driven well over a hundred miles apart from working in the shop. Probably I was overdoing things. After all, I was nearer fifty than forty and I drove myself pretty hard.

"Feeling better?" George was looking puzzled. "Never seen you look so exhausted. You drive yourself too hard, Anne. If you didn't enjoy your shop so much I'd tell you to sell the place, but I don't want you to give it up and then get bored."

I wish George didn't always think my thoughts.

"I was tired but I'm fine now. Think I'll have an early night. There's a sale at Little Watling tomorrow and I'd like to go. There'll be some lovely china and that always sells well."

George grinned. "I daren't suggest you sell that shop again. It isn't the profit you make but the pleasure of handling the stuff, isn't it?"

"You know me too well, and if I stayed at home all day what would I do? Mrs Gibson keeps this place spick and span and when you are writing I would drive you dotty. Of course I could come with you on your rambles but I'd probably take your mind from your job."

"Rubbish! I'd love it even after twenty years of being married to you!"

"I'll think about it, but I must get to that sale tomorrow."

"And if you sold the shop you would still want to go to auctions which we could never afford and the cottage would overflow with your finds!"

He was right. The shop had been my father's and it was in my blood.

"I'm off to bed."

"I'll bring you a hot drink."

But I was asleep when George came up and I slept without dreams. In the morning I was convinced the episode of the night before was because I had been exhausted.

Although it was October the really slack season had not yet begun. Our little market town is a great place for tourists. We've a lovely old manor house open to the public, an old castle and one of the most beautiful old churches in England, even if it is small. The square is charming and the houses and shops are all shapes and sizes. There's an ancient coaching inn on the opposite side of the square from my shop and it fills with Americans who spend hours in the old churchyard hopefully looking for the graves of long-dead ancestors. My shop does extremely well. It is one of the oldest buildings and so far the only antique shop.

The auction I was so set on attending was only twenty miles away but the items I wanted were towards the end of the catalogue so I had warned George I wasn't likely to be home before seven. I told Alice I would go straight home leaving her to close up.

I bought some rather nice china and quite a lot of copper pots and pans and was on the point of leaving when I spotted a box full of odds and ends from the kitchen. In it were some old flat-irons. Well worth waiting for. In case you don't know, old-fashioned flat-irons are a rage for using as doorstops. Then, at the last moment some old steel fire-irons! I packed everything in the car and then spotted the carved head. I had forgotten to give it to George. Taking it from the back I put it on the seat by my side, determined not to forget it tonight.

I wasn't tired. In fact I had never felt more fit and could have driven for miles. At least I wasn't likely to fall asleep at the wheel tonight!

Poor old George, I thought, as I drove along our road, he'll get fed up with doing the cooking. Not to worry, I'll get home early tomorrow. I was nearing the bend as I thought of it.

The headlights glared as the car came round the corner. This time I knew it was for real. Terror gripped me as I jammed on the brakes and turned the wheel. Into the hedge, into anything to avoid that racing car. It was too late. Again I felt the impact and heard the shattering glass and heard Harry Jones speaking. This time there was no mistake. I was dead. I heard Harry say so. Once again I came out of the terrifying experience and pulled myself together. I looked at my watch. Ten past seven. Exactly the same time as before. I didn't get out of the car. There was no need. I knew I should find nothing.

I waited until I was no longer shaking and pinched my cheeks to bring some colour to them. There was something definitely wrong with me. I had read of cases in which mental disorders cause the most peculiar hallucinations. I searched my brain to think of any other queer tricks my imagination had played, but could think of none. There must be a reason, something which triggered off that terrifying experience. I must talk to someone about it, but not to George. He'd pack me off to our doctor.

By the time I went into the cottage I had pulled myself together and had the carved head in my arms to take attention from myself.

I handed it to George and summoned a grin.

"I bought it yesterday but I was so confoundedly tired I forgot to bring it in. What do you think of it?"

He took the wrappings off and held it in the light.

"What a lovely piece of work. African I should think. So much wisdom in the face. As if there is a complete knowledge of life and death. Any idea of its value?"

"Not a clue. One reason for bringing it home, apart from the fact that I thought you would like it."

"I'll put it in the study. Who knows, that wise old face might inspire my new book."

Again I slept soundly, untroubled by dreams. It was Wednesday and I intended to get home early.

"Five-thirty at the latest," I said as I kissed George goodbye. "I'll cook supper and we'll have a lovely lazy evening watching TV."

But there was something I had to do. Talk to someone. Not our doctor. Old Dr Berry had known me all my life and would give me a lecture on overwork and a prescription for a tonic. His young partner would pack me off to see a psychiatrist. All I wanted was someone with plain common sense.

Mid-morning I went to see the Rev. Charles Honeyball. He is an old friend of ours and wise above average. I told him

153

undramatically just what had happened. He didn't seem to think me a nut-case.

"You've lived there about five years, haven't you, Anne? Ever heard of an accident taking place there, because I haven't?"

I shook my head. "The road is used so little except by the Millers and Harry Jones and his wife. I know it is a short cut to Planton, but not that short, and beyond the farm it's in a shocking condition."

"And you've never had an experience of this sort before?"

"Never."

"And it happened at exactly the same time each evening? Have you ever gone home at that time before?"

"Often. Twice last week I got home at quarter past seven. I must have reached that spot at about the same time as last night and the night before. Tonight I am going home early."

"You do that and try to put it out of your mind. I'll make a few inquiries, and don't get it into your head there is anything wrong with you."

When I got back to the shop we had an unusual customer. A tall, charming American, but that is not why he was unusual. He said he was particularly interested in African carvings. Had we any? I told him about the head and said my husband thought it was African. Could he see it? I explained it was at home and I didn't want to sell it, but if he was staying in the town I would bring it in the following morning and would be glad if he could tell me anything about it.

I was home before six to find George in a state of boyish excitement. George is a big man with a crop of untamable white hair and a pair of grey eyes that have never lost the eagerness of youth.

"Anne, who do you think phoned? Alex Mackay. He wanted to know if he could spend a few days with us and I said he could. Is that all right?"

"Of course it is. You'll have the time of your life together." Alex is an old colleague of George's. He stays with us whenever possible.

"He hasn't a car with him. He's just back from the States. He arrives about six-fifteen tomorrow and I said you would meet him. Didn't seem much point in me going to town as you will be there. I'll get the supper."

I covered a smile. George has a car but never drives into town if he can avoid it. He uses it to drive farther into the country. The look he gave me was as innocent as a babe. I told him about the American and said I was taking the head in to show him.

"Oh, good, I'd like to know something about him. The old boy positively smiles at me when I am working."

"Honestly, George, you are an idiot. Talk about letting your imagination run riot!"

In the morning I took the head with me. George was right, there was a hint of a smile on the perfectly carved mouth which I hadn't noticed before.

The American, whose name was Hannay, took the head gently in his long, thin hands. Everything about Mr Hannay was long and thin. The perfect Uncle Sam, including the neat, goatee beard. He stroked the head gently, feeling the hollows in the cheeks and running the tip of his index finger down the broad nose.

"It's African. From a small tribe who did most exquisite carving. Unfortunately there are few carvers left in the tribe. Are you sure you don't want to sell?"

"Positive. My husband has taken a fancy to it."

He gave a sudden smile. "I might as well own up. I knew the old boy who owned this but I was too late for the sale so they gave me your address. John used to swear this was the carving of an old witch doctor and had magical powers. I told him it looks more like a church elder. Positively benign."

"My husband says he smiles at him. I think he looks wise. Perhaps we see what we want to see!"

"Perhaps!"

Mr Hannay bought a nice old sampler for his wife. He gave

155

me an address in Philadelphia and said he would see me again next time he was in England. I wrapped up the head and put it back in the car.

The train was a few minutes late but seeing Alex again was a joy. He's a little man with a gnomelike face and dark brown eyes. Anyone less like George it would be impossible to meet, yet they are both crazy naturalists and very close friends.

Alex put his suitcase in the boot. I looked at my watch. We should arrive at the bend in the road at the same time as I had on those other two evenings.

"Alex, be an angel and drive. I know you like driving and I'm a bit tired."

"Bless you. You know I prefer to drive than be driven."

As we reached the bend I saw the lights, felt the impact and my head slumped forward. Alex stopped the car and put his arm round me.

"Anne, what's wrong? Are you ill?"

I pulled myself together. Alex's arm steadied me. I hadn't heard Harry's voice but I was shaking like a leaf.

"No, I just had an off sensation as we reached the bend. I'm all right now, honestly. Alex, please don't say anything to George."

It took a bit of persuading for he was convinced I was ill.

"Thank God you asked me to drive. Have you seen a doctor?"

"No, and I can assure you I'm not ill. Like you I am unused to being driven."

"You shouldn't drive until you've seen one."

Arguing with Alex pulled me together more than anything else could have done and I threatened him with murder and sudden death if he mentioned it to George.

Actually they were so pleased to see each other I think it went out of his head. It was George who spoke of Charles Honeyball.

"I'll see if he can come to dinner on Saturday," I said. "I'll collect him and take him back. There's something wrong with his car." Alex had obviously forgotten the incident on the road, but I hadn't, and I had to see Charles Honeyball before he saw Alex.

I went along to the rectory on Friday morning. I explained what had happened and this time I told him about the head.

"Alex saw nothing. He thought I was ill and a nice job I had persuading him not to tell George. It's something to do with that head, I know it is. I've driven along that road hundreds of times just after seven and nothing strange has ever happened. I'll bring the head with me tomorrow if you will drive. I told a thundering big lie and said your car was in dock. Funny, the words came so quickly and I'm not usually good at thinking something up on the spur of the moment."

"But Anne, my car *is* in dock!"

We stared at each other in something close to consternation.

We arranged to reach the bend about ten-past seven. Alex had seen and heard nothing. I wanted to know if Charles would. I took the head without saying anything to George.

We reached the lane and slowed down as we were a little early. Charles was at the wheel, for I dared not trust myself with a passenger by my side. Suddenly from behind us came the light of another car, coming at far too high a speed for such a narrow road. Charles drew into the side as it passed and muttered something which was far from polite about idiots driving. It was close to the bend. I saw the other headlights. There was a terrific crash, the shattering of glass and a high-pitched scream. Charles stopped the car and got out. I followed. I could hear running footsteps and, as we neared the crash I heard Harry Jones say, "This one's dead. I'll have a look at the other one."

Charles said, "Go and call an ambulance and the police, Anne. I'll wait here, then you go on home."

I called from Harry's cottage. Molly, Harry's wife, walked home with me. My legs were still shaking but I managed to get to the bathroom before I was violently sick. Did the girl I would never know take my place? Did the head give me temporary second sight, and if so why didn't Alex experience it? I shall never know the answer.

The head is still on the shelf in George's study, and I often touch it gently, but nothing would make me take it in the car again. I don't want to know what the future holds, thank you.